Close Shave

Elspeth crossed the porch and raised her hand to knock on the door. Longarm came flying after her. He launched himself forward, one arm hooking around her waist and his revolver in the other hand. Longarm took her down with him onto the porch floor. Three shots rang out from inside the house and splinters were blown out of the front door. Longarm was lying stretched full-length on the porch, Elspeth Palmer partially under him.

"Lemme get you out o' here," Longarm said. "Can you crawl on your hands an' knees? Just follow me, ma'am."

He rolled onto his back and tilted up the muzzle of his Colt as a man showed himself in the window. The outlaw was young and clean-shaven and he had a large-caliber revolver in this hand. That was all Longarm had time to see. He triggered a shot intended for the fellow's chest. The slug flew high, entering the underside of the man's chin and blowing on through the top of his skull. The bullet took an awful lot of brain and blood with it.

A second gunman leaped to the same window. Longarm fired. Dust puffed from the front of the man's shirt as two bullets tore into his chest, where his heart should be . . .

DON'T MISS THESE
ALL-ACTION WESTERN SERIES
FROM THE BERKLEY PUBLISHING GROUP

THE GUNSMITH by J. R. Roberts
Clint Adams was a legend among lawmen, outlaws, and ladies. They called him . . . the Gunsmith.

LONGARM by Tabor Evans
The popular long-running series about Deputy U.S. Marshal Long—his life, his loves, his fight for justice.

SLOCUM by Jake Logan
Today's longest-running action Western. John Slocum rides a deadly trail of hot blood and cold steel.

BUSHWHACKERS by B. J. Lanagan
An action-packed series by the creators of Longarm! The rousing adventures of the most brutal gang of cutthroats ever assembled—Quantrill's Raiders.

DIAMONDBACK by Guy Brewer
Dex Yancey is Diamondback, a Southern gentleman turned con man when his brother cheats him out of the family fortune. Ladies love him. Gamblers hate him. But nobody pulls one over on Dex . . .

WILDGUN by Jack Hanson
The blazing adventures of mountain man Will Barlow—from the creators of Longarm!

TEXAS TRACKER by Tom Calhoun
Meet J.T. Law: the most relentless—and dangerous—manhunter in all Texas. Where sheriffs and posses fail, he's the best man to bring in the most vicious outlaws—for a price.

TABOR EVANS

LONGARM

AND THE MIDNIGHT MISTRESS

JOVE BOOKS, NEW YORK

THE BERKLEY PUBLISHING GROUP
Published by the Penguin Group
Penguin Group (USA) Inc.
375 Hudson Street, New York, New York 10014, USA
Penguin Group (Canada), 90 Eglinton Avenue East, Suite 700, Toronto, Ontario M4P 2Y3, Canada
(a division of Pearson Penguin Canada Inc.)
Penguin Books Ltd., 80 Strand, London WC2R 0RL, England
Penguin Group Ireland, 25 St. Stephen's Green, Dublin 2, Ireland (a division of Penguin Books Ltd.)
Penguin Group (Australia), 250 Camberwell Road, Camberwell, Victoria 3124, Australia
(a division of Pearson Australia Group Pty. Ltd.)
Penguin Books India Pvt. Ltd., 11 Community Centre, Panchsheel Park, New Delhi—110 017, India
Penguin Group (NZ), Cnr. Airborne and Rosedale Roads, Albany, Auckland 1310, New Zealand
(a division of Pearson New Zealand Ltd.)
Penguin Books (South Africa) (Pty.) Ltd., 24 Sturdee Avenue, Rosebank, Johannesburg 2196,
South Africa

Penguin Books Ltd., Registered Offices: 80 Strand, London WC2R 0RL, England

This is a work of fiction. Names, characters, places, and incidents either are the product of the author's
imagination or are used fictitiously, and any resemblance to actual persons, living or dead, business
establishments, events, or locales is entirely coincidental.

LONGARM AND THE MIDNIGHT MISTRESS

A Jove Book / published by arrangement with the author

PRINTING HISTORY
Jove edition / November 2006

Copyright © 2006 by The Berkley Publishing Group.

ISBN: 0-515-14215-8

JOVE®
Jove Books are published by The Berkley Publishing Group,
a division of Penguin Group (USA) Inc.,
375 Hudson Street, New York, New York 10014.
JOVE is a registered trademark of Penguin Group (USA) Inc.
The "J" design is a trademark belonging to Penguin Group (USA) Inc.

PRINTED IN THE UNITED STATES OF AMERICA

10 9 8 7 6 5 4 3 2 1

Chapter 1

One truly handsome woman sat across the table from him. Silky black hair. Tiny waist but with an impressive swell of hip and breast on either side of that waist. Angelic face and a dimpled smile. This was their first social contact, lunch at the posh Stebbins Club, but Deputy United States Marshal Custis Long had every intention of seeing this lady again. In considerably less public circumstances.

The lady used a brilliantly white linen napkin to dab delicately at her lips then carefully folded it and laid it beside her place. "Thank you for the meal and the pleasant company, Custis."

"My pleasure," he told her. "But call me Longarm. All my friends do." A warm smile wrinkled the corners of his eyes.

"Are we to be friends then, Cus—I mean, Longarm?"

"I certainly hope so."

"That would mean becoming better acquainted," she said, looking down and toying with a spoon.

"Yes, I believe it would."

She looked up and met his gaze. "I would like that, Longarm."

"So would I," he admitted.

"Tonight?" she suggested.

"I thought you said . . ."

"I can cancel it," she very quickly replied.

Longarm's smile grew wider. "Tonight," he agreed. "I'll call for you."

"Yes."

"About seven?"

She hesitated. "My maid leaves at six. We could have dinner in. Make it six-thirty."

If his smile got any wider he was going to hurt himself. "Six-thirty," he repeated.

A waiter appeared at his elbow as if by magic—how the hell did they know these things?—and presented the bill, hidden within a leather folio. Longarm opened the folder, glanced at the amount and managed not to soil his britches. Eight dollars. *Eight* dollars! For two lousy meals. Well, all right, for two very good meals. But even so. Two meals. Eight bucks. What was the world coming to?

He reached into his trousers and extracted some change, selected a ten dollar gold eagle and slipped it inside the folio. The waiter accepted it with a raised eyebrow. Longarm scowled. Of course he wanted change back from the ten. Did the man think he was swimming in money? Good Lord, the cheek of people nowadays.

The man brought Longarm's change and the tall deputy left a perfectly respectable twenty-five cent tip, then stood and helped the lady with her shawl.

Six-thirty could not come soon enough.

He extended his elbow and assisted her out to find a hansom cab.

Longarm was whistling as he strolled along Colfax on his way to the gray stone federal building where U.S. Marshal

2

Billy Vail had his offices. He made a fine figure of a man on that late summer day, standing over six feet in height with broad shoulders and a flat belly over narrow hips.

His face was deeply tanned and he had a rather large handlebar mustache—damn thing needed trimming again but he just didn't have time for that at the moment. He had brown eyes and chestnut brown hair. He wore a tweed coat and brown corduroy trousers tucked into black cavalry boots, a flat-crowned brown Stetson hat, and he carried a double-action Colt revolver in a cross-draw rig high on his belly.

He was more craggy and rugged than handsome but women seemed to think him attractive enough . . . and then some. Men found him to be agreeable and easygoing—unless he had reason to cloud up and turn stormy.

He reached the federal building and quickly mounted the steps and went inside, letting himself into the marshal's office where the chief clerk looked up from his paper shuffling and frowned.

"You're late."

"Am I?" Longarm very carefully reached into his vest pocket and extracted a pear-shaped Ingersoll watch which he consulted before saying, "Henry, you're right again." Longarm grinned. "But I'm only a little late so why worry about it?"

"He wants to see you, that's why."

"About being a couple minutes late?" Longarm protested.

"More like thirty-five minutes. And anyway that is not what he wants to see you about. He has an assignment for you."

"Something quick an' easy, I hope. I got a date tonight."

"You *had* a date tonight," the bespectacled clerk corrected him. Henry, slightly built and with an inoffensive look

3

about him, had the appearance of a pushover. Which he was not. Henry had been known to pick up a revolver or a shotgun and lend assistance to the marshal whenever necessary. Longarm learned long ago that Henry could be as salty as anybody, never mind his wide-eyed innocent looks.

"Well whatever it is, dammit, it can wait until tomorrow."

"Not this time," Henry told him. "You'll . . . let the boss explain it. He knows more about it than I do anyway."

Longarm doubted that. Not much happened in or around this office that Henry did not learn about, one way or another.

"I'll tell him that you finally showed up." Henry got up from his desk and went to the closed door that led to Billy Vail's private office. He tapped lightly on it, waited for a moment and then let himself in, shutting the door again behind him.

Longarm shrugged. He crossed the room to the coat rack and placed his Stetson on one of the upright branches, then stood waiting to be ushered into the office of United States Marshal William Vail, Billy to his friends. And to a good many of his foes as well.

Long before he was appointed marshal of the department of justice's denver district he was a nail-spitting, hard-ass Texas Ranger with a reputation for accomplishing whatever he set out to do. That was what earned Billy his current job and it was the same attitude he saw in Deputy Custis Long. The two men got along well together.

Henry emerged from Billy's office after only a moment and held the door open. "You can go in now."

Longarm squared his shoulders and braced himself for a storm, then marched into the inner sanctum of law enforcement in this part of the country.

4

Chapter 2

"You're late," accused the bald, pink-cheeked United States marshal.

"Henry already mentioned somethin' about that, boss."

"There are people waiting for you."

"People?"

"Your assignment," Billy Vail said.

"Boss, I got a date tonight. Can't one of the other fellas take this one?"

"As a matter of fact, no, they can't. Everyone else is already busy with other work." Billy leaned back in his desk chair. The springs underneath it creaked in protest.

"Shit," Longarm grumbled.

Billy frowned and leaned forward, placing his hands palms down on the surface of his desk. "If the job is interfering with your social life, deputy, perhaps you should think about another line of work. Something that won't make so many demands on your time."

"Boss, I didn't mean . . ."

"I don't care what you meant. Or didn't mean," Vail said, his voice crisp, his expression cold.

"Yes, sir. I'm sorry."

5

"Now sit down and pay attention."

"Yes, sir." Longarm shifted one of the straight-backed office chairs to an angle that he liked and sat. He considered reaching into his coat for a cheroot but decided against it. He had already gotten Billy pissed off quite enough without adding that, too. He crossed his legs, folded his arms . . . and kept his mouth closed. Billy Vail was *not* in a good mood right now.

"I am sure you are familiar with the Honorable Howard Palmer," Vail said.

"I've never met him," the tall deputy responded, "but I've sure as hell heard of him. Who in this country hasn't?" Longarm was practically aching for a cheroot. Dammit.

"His work has given him a certain . . . notoriety, you might say," Billy said.

"That's one way o' putting it," Longarm agreed. One very understated way.

Palmer—Longarm could not remember exactly which of the northeastern states the congressman came from—was rallying support in the U.S. House of Representatives for bills that would make sweeping changes in the way the United States treated its Indian residents. The most controversial measure in Palmer's proposals called for a declaration that Indian land holdings in the future would be considered to be separate and apart from the United States and not subject to U.S. government controls, governance or regulation. The Indian tribes who owned those lands would be expected to govern and regulate them. Further, no encroachment upon or annexation by the U.S. government would be permitted. The current system of creating reservations would be wholly abandoned in favor of Indian self-governance and ownership.

Palmer had the enthusiastic support of the religious institutions in the northeast and to a lesser extent elsewhere in the country. He was vehemently opposed, however, by businessmen and political office holders from the Western states and territories.

Mining, logging and shipping magnates were said to practically foam at the mouth in their hatred for the congressman. If he were to prove successful in lining up the bleeding hearts—their term, not Longarm's, as quoted in the newspapers—to secure passage of Congressman Palmer's proposals, those businessmen would be severely hurt. Their use of Indian lands, if any, would have to be by negotiation instead of demand.

At best their profits would be reduced. At worst they might actually be evicted from lands rich in timber and minerals. Less production would mean less need for ships and railroad cars to carry those very bulky products. There would be fewer jobs available and lowered income for corporate shareholders throughout the country.

Longarm could see valid arguments on both sides of the question but took no stance on either. That was not his job. Thank goodness.

"What does this have t' do with me an' my assignment, boss?" He uncrossed his legs and absentmindedly reached into his coat for a cheroot, then realized what he was doing and brought his hand back down to his lap without the cigar.

"Threats have been made against the life of the congressman, Longarm. Threats that are being taken very seriously in Washington," Vail answered.

"That's in Washington. So what is . . ."

"Be patient. I'm trying to tell you."

"Yes, sir."

"The attorney general and the department of justice find these threats to be credible. Worrisomely so. They have asked Congressman Palmer to cancel his public appearances for the next few months, and he has agreed to do so. They have also assigned protective measures for him from the Secret Service."

"That sounds reasonable enough," Longarm said.

"And so it is," Billy agreed. "As far as it goes anyway. That protection, however, does not extend to his family. Which is where you come in."

"Me? What the hell do I have t' do with this?"

"That is what I've been trying to get to, Longarm, so be quiet and pay attention."

"Yes, sir."

"You may already know about Mrs. Palmer," Billy said.

"I've seen mention of her in the newspapers o' course. Sounds like a real fire-breathin' dragon woman."

"Not how I would have put it but . . . yes. The lady is, shall we say, outspoken."

"Outspoken an' then some," Longarm said. "Loudmouth is more like it. Her and her suffrage movement . . . I swear, Billy, they're worse 'n the temperance crowd." He snorted in derision. "Givin' women the vote. Craziest damn thing I ever heard."

"Then brace yourself because you are going to hear a great deal more about it."

"How's that, boss?"

"Because your assignment is to guard Mrs. Palmer and her little girl."

Longarm's eyebrows went up. He uncrossed his legs and leaned forward to listen more closely. Marshal Vail had Longarm's full attention now. "Me, boss? Shouldn't the

Secret Service or the government or somebody be the ones doin' that?"

"Deputy Long, you *are* the government. At least so far as this detail is concerned. The Secret Service is not authorized to give protection to the family members of congressmen. I gather they had to stretch the rules to get protection for the congressman, never mind his wife and little girl."

"I still don't see where I come in," Longarm grumbled.

"Mrs. Palmer and her daughter will be traveling in Wyoming and Colorado and points west for a series of speaking engagements. You will guard them."

"Have they been threatened, too?"

"Not specifically but it is assumed that the threats to Congressman Palmer could carry over to his family, especially since Mrs. Palmer is already, um . . ."

"Hated might be the word you're lookin' for, Billy. Hated. Reviled. All that sorta shit."

"Uh, yes," Billy said. "That would apply and a great deal more. The lady's message is not welcome, and it is very likely that she won't be either, with or without the threats to her husband."

"You say she's coming West?"

"They are already on the way."

"And I have t' watch out for 'em?"

"That's right."

"Wouldn't it be better t' assign a squad o' cavalry to play nursemaid to them, Billy? It'd be safer than having just one man do the job. More efficient, too. Some sons o' bitches see a wall o' blue between them an' the lady, they'd think twice about starting anything."

"That was already proposed, Longarm, and rejected."

"The army wouldn't go along with it?"

9

"Oh, the army would have. They would love to do something that might earn them the congressman's gratitude. The rejection came from Mrs. Palmer. She insists she does not want to appear fearful. She says that is not a message that would be compatible with her mission. She says she will permit no more than one man as a guard and furthermore he must not be in any sort of uniform. He must be inconspicuous. People should see him as a traveling companion rather than a guard."

"Sounds stupid t' me, boss. If she's a target, the cavalry would give her more protection than any one man possibly could."

"You are welcome to dislike the plan, Custis, but make no mistake about it. That *is* the plan. You have been assigned to guard Mrs. Palmer and her daughter."

"Shit," Longarm said. He reached inside his coat for that cheroot, pulled one out and began the process of preparing and lighting it.

"The railroad has laid on a special car for them to travel in and will arrange for a carriage at each of the scheduled stops."

"Trying t' curry favor with the congressman," Longarm said.

"Probably, but that is not my point."

"An' that would be . . . ?"

"They arrive here on the four-twenty. That is why I was concerned about you being late getting back from lunch. I was afraid you might not be able to meet them at the station.

"They have a dinner scheduled this evening with the Mile High Suffragettes. You will be in attendance, by the way; the meeting is not open to the general public but it has been publicized. Then you pull out for Cheyenne tomorrow morning at seven forty-two."

Longarm spat the end twist of tobacco into the palm of his hand then struck a lucifer aflame and lighted his cheroot. Damn but he was going to hate having to break that engagement this evening.

Chapter 3

There was something about a train station. It always made Longarm feel good. Eager and excited and alive. Even when he was only meeting someone and not heading out himself he could feel the excitement of all the travelers who were scurrying back and forth around him.

The smell had something to do with it, too, a scent that was unique to train stations but common to all of them wherever they were. It was a combination of coal smoke and cinders and soot, sharp in the nose and as pervasive and lingering as was the smoke from burnt gunpowder.

If the truth be known, Longarm enjoyed the atmosphere of a busy railroad station.

He paid the driver of the cab that had brought him from downtown—no point in having to pay extra to have this particular cab wait around; there would always be another available—and went inside the station. He checked with the clerk to make sure the 4:20 was on time, then borrowed a slip of paper and wrote out an apology to his lady friend.

"Boy!"

"Yes, sir?"

"I want this note delivered to the lady at this address,"

he said, showing the folded paper to the kid wearing a messenger cap. "Can you do that?"

"It's pretty far away, mister. It'd cost you."

"How much?"

"Twenty-five cents?" The tone of the boy's voice said quite plainly that he would be willing to negotiate down from that asking price if the customer balked at paying so much.

"Twenty-five is fine," Longarm told him, probably making the kid's day. He handed over the note and a quarter, then sweetened the deal with a five-cent tip.

"Gee, thanks, mister. I'll take it right away." The kid turned and started loping away.

"Hey, how come you're going that way?" Longarm called after him. "The exit you want is over there."

"Yes, sir, but my bicycle is over here. Don't worry, mister. I know where I'm going."

Longarm hoped that was so. He turned and put all thoughts of the dark-haired lovely, pleasant though they might be, out of mind. Right now he had other things to worry about.

Not that he really expected any attempts to be made on the lives of Mrs. Palmer and the congressman's little girl. But the possibility did exist. It was up to him to see that no harm came to them while they were visiting here.

It was not a job that he liked nor one he would have chosen for himself, but it was his nonetheless and he intended to see it through to the best of his ability. Dammit!

Just as a routine precaution he strolled slowly through the station and along the platform, seemingly aimless and inattentive. In fact he was very carefully looking over the people in the crowd, station employees, too, searching for any likelihood of threats. He saw nothing and no one to excite his interest.

And that was the way he damn sure wanted to keep it.

Finally he found a stout post to lean against, crossed his boots at the ankle and took his time about lighting a cheroot.

That cigar was long gone and another one half-smoked before a boy came through to announce the arrival of the 4:20. Out of idle curiosity Longarm pulled his Ingersoll from his vest pocket and checked the time. It was 5:17. And the 4:20 was just now coming into sight.

Efficiency, Longarm thought sourly. Yeah, right.

He looked again at the people who were rushing to meet the train. No one caught his attention. If anyone had evil designs on the lady and her daughter they must have been disguised mighty damned well. That nanny pushing the perambulator over there? Or the sub-teenage ragamuffins placing pennies on the rails for the locomotive to crush flat? He didn't think so.

Longarm took one last, satisfying drag on his cheroot and tossed it away on the ballast between the rails.

It was time to go to work.

Mrs. Palmer was pretty much what one would expect of a congressman's wife: she seemed like a smug, self-important, overdressed bitch.

She had powder packed so thick on her cheeks that she looked like she was wearing a mask. Actually, Longarm thought, she would have been a helluva lot better looking if she did have on a fright mask. At least then she would have an excuse to look so wild-eyed and hard.

Longarm had faced murderers with gentler and more likeable countenances than Mrs. Elspeth Fahrquar Palmer's.

She wore her graying hair piled high and tight, as intimidating as a knight's steel helm, and she carried a huge, puffy muff in the crook of her elbow.

Even though she was just stepping off a train ride that must have lasted for days there was the crackle of starched petticoats rustling beneath the skirts of her beaded gown with every step she took. Petticoats were the only thing that was ever likely to be under those skirts, Longarm figured. The amazement to him was how her husband had managed to beget a child upon her.

The poor son of a bitch must've been desperate, Longarm figured. And blind drunk at the same time.

Lordy but the woman was ugly. Long ear lobes. Huge, hooked nose like a Lebanese street peddler. Bulging eyes. Lips so thin they could hardly be seen.

And all that powder. Jeez!

The Palmers' little girl, on the other hand . . .

Glenda Palmer was, in short, a knockout.

Longarm guessed her age at about nineteen or twenty. Blond. Petite. Stacked. With a face that must have been modeled direct from one of the Maker's angels.

She wore no makeup, and she needed none. She had soft brown eyes and a blush on her cheeks.

Longarm doubted he had ever seen a mother and daughter so dissimilar. And some fools claim if you want to know what a girl will look like when she ages then look at her mother. Ha! There was no way in this world that Glenda Palmer could ever end up looking like her mother Elspeth. No way at all, Longarm would've put money on that and called it as sure a bet as he'd ever taken.

Glenda was a peach, her mother a pit. Go figure.

Longarm introduced himself and gave instructions to

16

the entourage of porters wheeling the ladies' trunks and one small maid who was carrying a stack of hat boxes.

"This way everyone. We'll get a cab . . ." He looked behind the Palmers and amended that. "Or maybe two, an' get you checked into your hotel. There's rooms for you at the Carlton House, same place as your meeting tonight with the suffragettes."

"Will you be with us throughout the tour, Mr. Long?" Glenda asked, her eyes bright and her smile warm.

Longarm could not help but feel a stir of interest. The girl was young. But not *too* young. Oh no, she was not too young. No, sir, not at all. "I'll be with you for as long as you need me, Miss Palmer."

The girl's smile seemed shy and secretive, and it held what might well have been a hint of promise.

"Hurry up," the mother snapped. "We haven't time to dawdle."

"Yes, ma'am." Longarm motioned for the porters to follow and offered his elbow to Mrs. Palmer; Glenda, the maid and the porters all trailed along behind as he led the way to the taxi stand.

Chapter 4

Longarm pitied the Honorable Howard Palmer. If dinner conversation was anything to go by, the gentleman was required to listen to a constant and unrelenting barrage of women's suffrage claptrap.

It was "women this" and "women that," and if any mention of the male of the species did manage to sneak in it was only so Elspeth Palmer could point out how cruel and thoughtless and selfish and foul men invariably were.

And it didn't help a damn thing that they were surrounded by forty or fifty of Denver's like-minded matrons, most of whom were as butt ugly as Mrs. Palmer. Longarm swore he had never seen a homelier crowd of females, not even the filthy, impoverished, snaggle-toothed women of the Digger Indian clans over in Nevada.

As a matter of fact he could see a fair number of comparisons between these ladies and the Indian squaws.

Since he was given absolutely no opportunity to so much as say a word and might well have been mobbed by a horde of angry women if he had opened his mouth, he had more than ample time to sit there and make mental note of how many comparisons there were.

The squaws were dirt-encrusted, scrawny creatures who had spent their lives living one handful of bugs above utter starvation. The suffragettes of Denver were leathery and dry with pinched mouths and a flinty demeanor.

How any man could allow his wife . . . Longarm shook his head. The whole damn thing was beyond his understanding.

By the time dessert rolled around he felt an urge to take a razor strop to the backsides of each and every one of them. Starting with Mrs. Palmer. It was only his keen sense of duty—and the fact that these harridans scared the bejabbers out of him—that kept him from making a scene.

Or anyway kept him there. Slipping out, if only for a smoke, would have been almighty welcome. But he had a job to do, and it would be a mite difficult to explain to the boss that, sorry, he wasn't there when an assassin or a kidnapper showed up because he was outside puking over what these examples of the fairer sex were discussing over dinner.

Glenda, on the other hand, was an entirely different matter. She had "freshened up" and changed clothing after they settled into their suite of rooms, and she looked far more delectably edible than anything on the menu.

She was wearing a close-fitting gown of some light blue fabric. Her hair was a cascade of tight curls, and her mouth was as soft and full and generous as her mother's was parsimonious and forbidding.

The girl was a toothsome morsel, no doubt about it, and under other circumstances . . .

Longarm sighed. These were *not* other circumstances. He had a job to do. And while he might normally be inclined to say it would be a blessing if some son of a bitch did sneak in and put Elspeth Palmer out of her misery—

and everybody else's—he would not be meaning that in the literal sense. He had to admit that murder was wrong. Even when it was a shrill biddy like one of these that was being murdered.

It was kinda tempting though.

Longarm sighed and contented himself with thoughts of that nature, all the while seeking anything out of the ordinary among the waiters and few other males who happened to be in sight.

It was one long son of a bitch of a meal though.

And to think . . . he could have been spending his evening in the company of just one dark-haired lovely woman.

Damn!

He sighed again and had a swallow of water, having to practically sit on his hands to keep from reaching inside his coat for a cheroot.

Damn, indeed.

Chapter 5

Oh, shit! What was that fellow doing skulking around by the door leading into the hotel kitchen?

He was a mousy little son of a bitch with hair that was growing in clumps and patches. He had a pinched face and sharp, pointed nose. His suit was threadbare and fit him badly over narrow shoulders and a sunken chest. All in all he was a poor specimen of the human male.

He might have been the sort of unmanly man who Longarm might expect to see at a suffrage seminar. But his actions were suspicious indeed.

For one thing, Longarm was fairly sure the fellow had emerged from the kitchen instead of the lobby.

And he kept turning around to stand facing away from the roomful of women. Whenever he did that his shoulders hunched even closer together than they normally were and he bent forward. Longarm could not see for sure but he thought the scruffy little man was reaching inside his coat whenever he turned around like that. Yet he had nothing in his hands when he turned to face the dining room.

Suspicions fully aroused, Longarm murmured an excuse and quietly left the table.

He did not want to approach the fellow directly. That could lead to a shooting scrape, and Longarm figured the last thing they needed was to have bullets flying around all these women.

He went out into the lobby as if seeking the crapper but as soon as he was out of sight from the dining area, he stretched his legs and commenced to hurry.

"Quick," he said, grabbing a bellboy by the arm. "How do I get to the kitchen without goin' through that room there?"

The boy gave him a startled look and swallowed hard.

"It's all right, son. I'm a deputy United States marshal."

"Really? Can I see your gun?"

"Later maybe. Now how do I get t' the damn kitchen?"

The boy looked disappointed. He sighed and said, "Down that little hallway beside the clerk's desk. You see there? All the way to the end. It's the door on the left."

Longarm let go of the kid and loped swiftly toward the back of the hotel. He shoved the door open and stepped into the kitchen, his Colt already in hand.

A staff of probably a dozen people, cooks in white smocks and mushroom-shaped floppy hats and waitresses in black uniforms and white aprons, were dashing back and forth performing chores that Longarm could not begin to comprehend. It all looked like chaos to him as the staff tried to cope with the food orders from the regular guests and at the same time get out dessert trays for all those women's suffrage lunatics.

The place was a cacophony of smells, not all of them good ones. Roasting meat and hot grease and the sharp scent of naphtha soap dominating the rest.

It was almighty noisy as well with the clang of pot lids and bang of skillets and the yammer of waitresses calling out food orders, although who would be listening and how they would keep it all straight Longarm could not imagine.

The kitchen seemed to be in a completely different world from the order and elegance shown in the dining room only a few paces distant.

"You," Longarm snarled, taking one of the white-coated cooks by the elbow. "Where . . . never mind, thanks." He pushed the cook away and headed for the side door where he'd gotten a glimpse of the little fellow in the ill-fitting tweed suit.

Eyes flashing and gun in hand he crossed the kitchen in long, swift strides. He stood behind the door where his quarry was, took a deep breath and with a scowl shouldered the door ajar.

Oh, shit, he repeated to himself.

But for a far different reason this time. The little SOB was no murderer with a political ax to grind.

He was a damn reporter of some sort. Had to be.

It was not a pistol he kept reaching into his coat for. It was a notepad. Whenever he turned away from the dining hall it was so he could hunch protectively over that pad while he scrawled notes in it with a stub of lead pencil.

Longarm slid his big .45 back into its holster, then reached out and grabbed the little weasel by the coat collar. He would have preferred taking him by the scruff of the neck and giving him a good shaking, but he dragged the surprised little man . . . or boy—he seemed barely old enough to shave and somewhat short of actual manhood— into the steamy, overheated kitchen.

"This meeting is closed to the press," Longarm snarled. Not that he gave a damn about that himself, but the little man had given him a start and he was feeling more than a little peevish because of it.

"I have a right to be here," the fellow blustered.

"No, dammit, you don't. Not unless they say you do. It's their meeting an' it's not open to the public."

"They sold tickets. That makes it public," the reporter insisted.

"Did you buy one?" Longarm shot back at him.

The fellow did not answer that, which Longarm figured was more than answer enough.

"Get out o' here," Longarm snarled.

"I won't. You can't make me."

Longarm almost laughed in his face. Except that he would have had to drop down to his knees to get to the fellow's face level. He could not have been more than five foot four, Longarm thought, and the tall deputy towered head and shoulders over him. "Wanna bet?"

"If you touch me, I'll call a cop," the reporter threatened.

"I am touching you, asshole." Longarm gave the fellow's coat collar a bit of a shake to remind him of the fact. "An' besides, I am a cop, a deputy U.S. marshal. Now who the hell are you?"

"How do I know you're a marshal?"

"Because I said so. Are you gonna tell me who you are?"

The fellow pulled himself up to his full height, such as it was, and puffed his chest out. "I am Sebastian Brewer." He hesitated, then added, "I am a writer."

Longarm noticed that Brewer did not mention which newspaper he wrote for. If any. Likely he was not employed by any newspaper or magazine although it was possible he sold snippets of his writing here or there as occasion arose. Longarm did not care enough to press him about it anyway.

"Good for you, asshole. I'm sure your mother's proud. But you gotta get your butt outta here."

"I will not."

Longarm sighed. Then he turned Sebastian Brewer around so that he was facing away from him. Bending his legs to a crouch, Longarm reached around, took a good hold on Brewer's waist, then straightened up and lifted. Longarm picked Brewer up with no more effort than if he were a department store mannequin.

"Hey!"

Longarm paid no attention to the little fellow's protests. He carried Brewer kicking and squirming through the kitchen.

"Back door's over there? Thank you."

He pushed the door open, deposited Brewer in a trash-strewn alley beside some very smelly refuse bins, and said, "Don't come back. Next time I might arrest you." It was an empty threat. Brewer had violated no federal law that Longarm knew of. But Brewer did not have to know that.

Longarm turned and went back into the kitchen, leaving Brewer fuming in the stink of the alley.

Chapter 6

"We shall go to the hospitality suite for coffee now," the old battle-ax told him. "You may accompany us."

Damned nice of her to offer, Longarm thought. Since he'd play hell trying to guard someone he wasn't with, he silently grumbled. He supposed his displeasure with this whole affair showed. He really did not give a shit. "Wherever you go," he said, "it's my job t' be there, too."

The congressman's wife gave him a long look that he could not begin to interpret, then turned and said something to the head of the local suffragette movement. That woman—Longarm had not caught her name and did not care—was as butt ugly as was Mrs. Palmer. It was one helluva crowd, these suffragettes. A joy to be with. Yeah, right.

The Denver woman laughed at whatever it was Mrs. Palmer said to her, then Mrs. Palmer turned and with her nose in the air marched out into the lobby and up the stairs. Longarm followed sullenly behind, all the more unhappy when he realized that Glenda was not coming with them. The daughter was the only bright spot in the crowd. A lily among a bunch of cacti.

Why the hell couldn't Billy have given this chore to Dutch or Smiley or one of the younger boys?

The gaggle of females—Mrs. Palmer and four locals—headed for the stairs leading to the guest rooms on the upper floors.

Longarm caught up with them and touched Mrs. Palmer on the elbow to get her attention. He kept his voice low and said, "Excuse me, ma'am, but I can only watch your daughter when she's close by. Could you ask her to stay with you, please?"

The woman sniffed. "Glenda is a free woman with rights and a will of her own."

"Yes, ma'am, she surely is, but if I'm t' keep an eye on her . . ."

"Your job, sir, is to keep an eye on would-be assassins, *not* on Glenda or myself. Have you not been listening to the comments from these ladies and myself? My daughter is not chattel and never will be. She said she wants to take the air. It is her decision. Not mine. And it certainly is not yours, sir."

"But I can't . . ."

"I shall take the responsibility," Mrs. Palmer snapped. "Now please be so good as to do your job in silence, sir."

She would "take the responsibility" would she? Longarm thought bitterly. Yet if Glenda turned up missing or, worse, dead it would be Custis Long's neck on the chopping block, and a United States congressman damn sure had the power to wield the ax. Damn the man anyway for allowing his women to get so uppity.

Longarm generally sympathized with the women's rights crowd. It seemed only fair. But these particular women were sure capable of grating on a man's nerves.

"Yes, ma'am," was all he could say, though.

He had a choice. He could stick with Mrs. Palmer and do his best to cover her. Or he could go look for Glenda and try to keep an eye on her.

He had a choice . . . but not really. If there really did prove to be an assassination attempt—and the book was still out about that—it was much more likely that the congressman's wife would be the target. She was the one making a public spectacle of herself, so she was the more likely to be recognized. Glenda was just another pretty girl and no threat to anyone.

If he could only protect one of them, the wife pretty much had to be that one.

And there were witnesses to what Mrs. Palmer told him about Glenda's right to come and go as she pleased.

Fine! Dammit.

He trooped upstairs at a slight distance from the suffragettes. No one leaped out of any doorways or was skulking in the shadows. The women let themselves into a suite where a table was spread with wine and canapés. They removed their floppy hats—there seemed to be some element to this suffrage movement that lent itself to large hats—and poured themselves large glasses of some sort of red wine. Time to let their hair down, Longarm figured. Figuratively speaking that is.

The woman's voices buzzed with gossip and male-bashing jokes that Longarm had no interest in hearing. He found a corner as distant from the ladies as he could manage and settled down to wait.

An hour or so later the group broke apart, the local women heading off to their own homes while Mrs. Palmer imperiously beckoned Longarm to follow. She led the way up another flight of stairs to the suite that had been given to her for the overnight stay in Denver.

31

"You are dismissed," she said when she had the door open.

"I want t' take a look through the place before I leave you here," Longarm told her.

"Do you expect to see blackguards hiding under the beds?" she sniffed rather nastily.

"It just could be," he told her, making an effort to conceal his exasperation. "So I reckon we'll all of us sleep better if I look t' make sure before I leave."

"Very well. If you must." She moved aside to allow him entry.

Longarm was pleased and a little surprised, too, to find Glenda already in the sitting room with a magazine open in her lap and the lamp wick turned high. She looked up when he came in but did not offer a greeting or a smile.

" 'Scuse me, miss." He touched the brim of his Stetson and moved swiftly through the two-bedroom suite.

And he did look under the beds. Also in the wardrobes. It took only a few moments to satisfy himself that no one was hiding in there. He checked to see that the windows and the French doors were all closed against the night air and properly locked.

Finally, he nodded to Mrs. Palmer and told her, "I'll have t' go home tonight and get my bag and such. I'll call for you in the morning early enough that you can get some breakfast before we head for the train station. Please don't go downstairs nor anywhere outside these rooms before I get here."

"Aren't you being overly dramatic, deputy? These threats against my husband have nothing to do with me or my daughter."

"Ma'am, me and my boss would rather guard you when there's no danger than leave you alone when there is an attempt to harm you. Like they say, ma'am, better safe than sorry."

The woman only sniffed once more—it was a response she seemed to favor for many things—and showed him to the door.

Longarm stood outside for a moment until he heard the bolt slide closed behind him, then hurriedly pulled out a cheroot and lighted it. He was damn near perishing for want of a smoke after having to do without one throughout dinner. Once that was taken care of, and feeling a helluva lot better, he went downstairs to look for a cab. He needed to get a little sleep if he could, then grab his bag.

Damn these women anyway though.

Chapter 7

It was not yet dawn when Longarm returned to the hotel. His eyes felt gritty from lack of sleep, but he was washed and freshly shaved and wearing his best light brown tweed coat. And he was smoking like a chimney. He might not get another chance to light up for hours so he wanted to take advantage of the opportunity while he had it.

There was no one on duty at the desk. Either the clerk had been called away, or he had slipped inside the office to nap until he was needed. Or there was some other good reason.

It occurred to Longarm that a "good reason" might include being confronted by a gunman who wanted to know where Congressman Palmer's wife and daughter were quartered.

With that rather ugly thought in mind Longarm took the stairs in a rush. When he reached the Palmers' suite, the door was standing open. He felt a moment of heart-pounding concern. He reached the doorway and went in, Colt in hand and ready to fire.

Glenda was sitting calmly on a settee. Mrs. Palmer was standing nearby. Both were quite all right, and there were no assassins in view. The room did, however, reek of some sharp, floral scent.

"What the hell are you women doing leaving your door open like that?" he demanded. "Anybody wandering past could step inside and shoot you both down. I thought I told you . . ."

"You are not in command of us, deputy marshal whatever-your-name-is. We have agreed to allow you to accompany us, but you may most emphatically not tell us what to do. I am sure we are perfectly safe with or without your services, and as it happens Glenda spilled a bottle of perfume. We needed to air the room out. Either that or suffocate. Now if you don't mind, we shall ring to have our bags taken down and then proceed to breakfast. Will you be coming?" Damned old bitch had her nose hiked up so high that if a rain cloud came along, she would surely drown.

Glenda scowled at him, then gathered up her handbag and stood, her skirts rustling.

"Come, dear."

"Yes, Mama."

There was a brief pause while Mrs. Palmer gave several sharp, imperious tugs on the tasseled bell cord, then the ladies exited the suite, ignoring Longarm completely. He tagged meekly behind, never mind that he was unhappy with this situation or these people. He was not here to be happy about a single damned thing; he was here to do a job, and he figured to do exactly that to the very best of his abilities or anyway as close to that as these two snooty women would allow.

The three of them descended the stairs and headed for the guest dining room rather than the large banquet room where the suffragettes had met the evening before.

At breakfast Longarm was excluded from the mundane conversation between mother and daughter. That was all right with him. It meant he had plenty of time to wrap himself around a plate of ham and fried potatoes and to dip his mustache in several cups of excellent coffee before the ladies were done.

"You may bill my husband for our meals," Elspeth Palmer declared when they were finished with breakfast. She sniffed and pointed. "He can pay for his own."

She wasn't only a bitch, she was a cheap bitch, Longarm thought sourly. His expression showed none of that opinion though. He kept his face as neutral as if he were in a poker game.

He had no choice but to dig into his pocket and come up with a half dollar to cover the cost of his meal. He left that beside his plate, reminding himself to make a note of the expenditure so he could put it on his expense form later and get it back.

Longarm had arranged with the desk the evening before to have a cab to take them to the railroad depot. It was waiting outside with the luggage already loaded. Longarm grabbed the carpetbag that he'd left beside the desk on his way upstairs and added that to the ladies' things piled in the luggage boot.

By the time he was done with that, Mrs. Palmer had the carriage door firmly shut and was again in deep conversation with her daughter. Longarm never could understand how women could find so damn much to talk about. It sometimes seemed their mouths ran day and night. And not a bit of that of any real importance.

He took the closed door to mean that he was not really welcome inside the coach, so he stepped onto the axle and up into the driving box.

"Where to, guvnor?"

Longarm told him, then took a firm hold on the seat rail so he wasn't jolted off when the skittish horses, still fresh after spending the night in the barn, took off.

The sun was just beginning to lift itself over the horizon and the morning air was crisp and cold and smelled of coal smoke from countless breakfast fires in thousands of stoves throughout the city.

Chapter 8

"I will *not* sit in the smoking car just so you can satisfy your vulgar tastes, nor will I subject my daughter to those influences."

Longarm considered asking Mrs. Palmer exactly which evil influences she meant by that, the smoke or the people. But all he said was, "Yes, ma'am."

A moment later he added, "Excuse me, ma'am, but the train's over here. We need t' go this way, not . . . ma'am?"

The woman marched in her usual nose-high, tight-ass posture into the station with Glenda trailing behind wearing an expression of bored indifference.

"But . . . well, shit!" Longarm mumbled the last, then stretched his legs to catch up with the women. The damned train was almost loaded and would be pulling away from the platform in a few minutes.

"What do you mean I cannot?" Mrs. Palmer was demanding of the ticket agent when Longarm got there. "Do you know who I am? Now I insist . . ."

"Lady, there ain't no way we could hook on a special carriage this late even if we had one available, which we don't. Now if you want to ride to Cheyenne you can do it on that train out there, which you barely have time enough to catch if you hurry, or you can wait for that special coach, which I can get you by Sunday or thereabouts, or you can go talk to the stagecoach people, or you can rent a horse, or as far as I'm concerned you can walk. But you *cannot* have a private car just on the spur of the moment like that."

"My husband will hear about this poor service," Mrs. Palmer warned the harried ticket agent. "He sits in the United States Congress, and I intend to tell him."

"That's fair. I expect I'll tell my wife about it when I get home tonight, too, see what she thinks of just how stupid women from back East can be."

Mrs. Palmer swelled up so that she looked like she gained a good three inches over her normal height. "Well, I never!"

"Madam, maybe you ought to." The ticket agent turned away and busied himself with something away from the window. Longarm felt like applauding the guy. As it was, he had to maintain a straight face while he followed the Palmers out onto the platform again.

They were barely in time to reach a passenger coach before one of the crewmen pulled the steps up. The fellow hauled the women up, then snarled a little as Longarm clambered inside.

"We shall sit at the front," Mrs. Palmer declared.

"You might find there's a lot of cinders flyin' in that close to the engine, ma'am."

"We shall close the windows."

"Yes, ma'am." Longarm gave a sad glance toward the smoking car behind them, then trudged in the old witch's wake as she conducted a grand march toward the front of the train with Glenda close on her heels.

Once in the foremost car she surveyed the available

seats, then had the gall to ask some poor son of a bitch to move elsewhere so she could have his seat at the very front of the coach. The amazement, Longarm thought, was that he did it. The mousy little fellow bounced to his feet and bowed to the woman before scurrying away down the aisle. The woman had brass. Longarm had to give her that much.

The train lurched into motion a split second after Mrs. Palmer sat down; it was almost like the railroad had to have her permission before it could move, forcing Glenda to hurriedly plop herself into the seats facing her mother.

That left Longarm having to choose between sitting next to Mrs. Palmer and Glenda. His preference was clear, but so was his duty. He needed to be able to keep an eye down the length of the car. That meant sitting in a rear-facing seat. And that meant sitting beside Mrs. Palmer.

There certainly would be no pleasure in that.

On the plus side of the ledger, facing in that direction meant that he would be looking directly at Glenda throughout the journey. There were worse views that a man could have. The girl was mighty handsome with her hair pinned high and a rosy blush—painted there? was that possible?—on her cheeks.

If only he could have a cigar now. . . .

"Tickets. Tickets, please." The conductor came through, walking easily in imitation of a seaman's rolling gait as the car swayed and clattered north.

Mrs. Palmer showed the man some sort of pass. Congressional privilege, Longarm guessed. But then the railroads depended on the United States congress for the land grants that made their lines possible to begin with and on lucrative government contracts for mail and freight services after those roads were completed. He supposed it should be no surprise that the wife of Congressman Howard Palmer and her daughter rode free.

Just like he himself did. He showed the conductor his badge instead of a ticket.

Five or so minutes later Glenda stood up. Longarm assumed she needed the toilet. Instead she announced, "I'm going to one of the other cars. I'll see you when we get to Cheyenne."

"All right, dear." Mrs. Palmer said absently. She was engrossed in reading a pamphlet she had extracted from her purse and seemed to pay little attention to what her daughter said.

"Excuse me for intruding," Longarm put in, "but I wanta remind you that I can't keep an eye on both of you if you aren't together. Could you please stay here with you mother, miss?"

Glenda gave Longarm a look like he had just stood up in church and shouted obscenities. "How dare you!"

"Miss Palmer, please. All I'm tryin' . . ."

"Run along, dear," her mother said, and Glenda hurried away toward the rear of the train, passing out of their coach and on to the trailing cars.

"Ma'am, couldn't she just go t' the back of this coach if she wants some privacy? Let me go fetch her back up here. Please."

"I am sure you are trying to do your job, deputy, but I see no reason for all this alarm and excitement. Howard exaggerates. He always does. That is what political figures do, you know. Hyperbole is part of their trade. I learned a long time ago to pay no attention to it. Now please. Settle down. You may accompany us. I understand that. You have your orders. But we really do not require assistance from any male. And while I think about it, if you simply must remain here with me would you please move over to that seat." She pointed to the front-facing seat Glenda had just vacated.

"I can't do that, ma'am. I need t' be able to keep an eye on the other passengers. I can't do that properly if I'm facing this wall behind us."

"Oh, good grief! All right then. I shall move." Mrs. Palmer rolled her eyes and with a terribly put-upon look moved over to the front-facing seat then promptly resumed reading. Longarm might as well not have existed.

Thank you ever so fucking much, Billy Vail, Longarm thought sourly, his hand aching to slide inside his coat for a cheroot.

He supposed Mrs. Palmer would not mind in the slightest if he left her here while he went back to the smoking car for a few minutes. For a few minutes? Hell, she likely wouldn't mind if like Glenda he went back there and stayed for the duration of the trip.

And maybe the woman was right. Maybe there really was no threat.

Longarm was not going to take that chance though, never mind Mrs. Palmer's skepticism.

If Billy Vail said there was a threat, well, Custis Long was going to believe there was one. Period.

He wriggled sideways on the padded seat bench and wedged himself into the corner with his hat brim pulled down and his attention wandering while he kept an eye on the other passengers in Mrs. Palmer's car.

Chapter 9

The Cheyenne station had the same soot and cinders smell as the Denver depots, but in Cheyenne there was less in the way of smoke from coal cooking fires and more of the sharp, penetrating smell of cow manure from the loading pens nearby. And there was something too about the air in Cheyenne—in all of Wyoming Territory for that matter—something clean and fresh and open. Longarm liked Wyoming.

He helped Mrs. Palmer down onto the platform and took a deep breath, drinking in air that was laced with smoke and steam from the locomotive. He had his carpetbag in one hand and Mrs. Palmer—he could not help thinking of her as "the other bag"—on his other arm. There was no sign of Glenda.

"Where is . . . never mind, I see her."

Glenda descended gracefully from the last car in the train. She was on the arm of a young man who assisted her to the platform, bowed politely and hurried on about his business before Longarm could get a good look at him. Not that he seemed any sort of threat to the Palmer family. His actions were entirely proper and aboveboard.

"You know better than to go traipsing off by yourself

like that," Elspeth Palmer scolded as soon as Glenda was within range of her rather shrill voice.

"Oh, mama," Glenda said when she joined them. "I never get to spend time with anyone young."

"And you won't either, not until we return home. Now mind yourself, young lady, or I shall send you back to Mrs. Forsythe."

That was a name Longarm was not familiar with, but from the tone of the conversation he guessed the lady would be a nanny or a housekeeper or perhaps the head-mistress of a school for young ladies. Whoever and what-ever she was, it was obvious that Glenda would rather be here than back home in Mrs. Forsythe's charge.

"Yes, Mama."

"Do you have everything? Did you leave anything aboard the coach?"

"No, Mama."

"Well, thank goodness for small favors." Mrs. Palmer sniffed loudly, then gestured toward Longarm with her chin. "You may take us to the house now."

"And what house would that be, ma'am?"

"Do not be impertinent, young man."

"Miz Palmer, you haven't told me where you're goin'. I got no idea where t' take you."

"Oh." She sniffed again. "We shall be staying tonight at the Belton house."

"Is that the name of a hotel or . . ."

"Oh, for pity's sake. Do I have to do *every*thing?" El-speth Palmer evidently despaired of getting any assistance from Longarm. She took over herself, and led Longarm and Glenda back to the baggage car. She corralled a red-cap, identified her trunk and bags and had them loaded onto a hand cart. Then she gave instructions as to the precise handling she expected and where her things were to be delivered. Finally, she sniffed again and said, "Follow me."

Mrs. Palmer marched at the head of their little procession, she of course at the fore, Glenda close on her heels, Longarm behind Glenda's swaying skirts—the girl's ass wasn't half bad actually; it was round and firm and looked downright toothsome. At the rear was the porter who pushed the wheelbarrow-like luggage cart, whose wheels made a sustained crunching sound as they rolled over the cinders and gravel. The noise of the cart subsided to a low rumble once they got away from the depot and were traveling over dirt instead.

On the board sidewalk a block ahead Longarm saw someone step out of a storefront. He did not get a good look at the man because of Mrs. Palmer's and Glenda's huge, feather-bedecked hats obstructing his vision.

A moment later he discovered what it was that he had missed seeing.

"Oh!"

Mrs. Palmer shrieked.

Glenda fainted.

The sound of a gunshot boomed hollowly, shattering the quiet of a pleasant afternoon.

The redcap pushing the luggage cart grunted softly.

Longarm flung himself out from behind the women, his Colt already in hand and coming level.

At that distance it likely would do no good at all to fire quickly from the hip. The shooter was standing on the sidewalk with a revolver in hand. A halo of fire and white smoke burst out of the barrel even as Longarm brought his own gun up. The slug sizzled past somewhere overhead.

Longarm took careful aim on the bottom of the V where the fellow's vest buttoned together over his heart.

The big Colt roared and rocked back in his hand, and he thumbed the hammer back ready to squeeze off another shot.

The second shot was not needed. In the next block ahead, the shooter threw his arms high, not in surrender but as an involuntary reflex reacting to the bullet that struck him square in the chest. His revolver flew out of his hand and landed in the street a good twenty feet away before he dropped to his knees and then toppled face forward onto the gritty boards of the sidewalk.

Longarm stepped to Mrs. Palmer's side and wrapped an arm protectively around her shoulders before he turned, pistol held ready, to see if there were any other would-be assassins on the Cheyenne streets this day.

The streets for two blocks around were silent and suddenly empty except for Longarm's small party and the dead man lying sprawled facedown on the sidewalk ahead.

"Are you all right?"

"Yes, I think . . . Glenda. Are you all right, baby?"

"I'm okay, Mama. I wasn't . . . I'm all right."

Judging by the acrid stench that was in Longarm's nostrils at least one of the women was not quite completely all right. At least one of them, likely Glenda, had filled her drawers. That was all right. Shit washes off. Bullet wounds, unfortunately, do not.

Longarm turned to ask the porter if he was all right as well. There was no need to ask. The redcap, a middle-aged black man with graying hair and a sunny disposition, was lying crumpled between the poles of the handcart, blood seeping into the dirt beneath him.

"Wait here. Don't move, either one o' you." He hurried back to kneel beside the black man, but he was dead. The assassin's bullet had found a mark. Just not the right target. He had needlessly murdered an innocent man.

Longarm went back to the women, prepared to defend them if necessary, but there was no other threat in view.

In a few minutes folks began to move out onto the streets and sidewalks again. One of the first of them was a competent looking young man wearing the badge of a Cheyenne town constable. The constable held a sawed-off shotgun across his chest but did not threaten or bluster with it.

Longarm shoved his Colt back into its holster and spread his empty hands wide for the constable to see. "I'm gonna reach inside my coat now. I got a badge there, son. I'm a deputy U.S. marshal."

"That's all right. I know who you are. You're Long, right? The one they call Longarm?"

"That's right. Have we met before?"

"No, sir, but you was pointed out to me once when you was in Cheyenne. My name's Jason Gilmore."

Longarm shook hands with the young fellow. "Pleased to meet you, Jason. There ladies here are the wife an' daughter of Congressman Howard Palmer. There's been some threats against the congressman and I'm looking over them. I'd like t' get them off the street now if you wouldn't mind takin' over here. And gettin' another porter to bring their stuff over to . . . where is it that you're going, Miz Palmer?"

"The Belton house," she said weakly, her voice little more than a whisper.

"D'you know it?" Longarm asked Gilmore.

"If you mean banker Will Belton's house, sure."

Mrs. Palmer nodded. "That is . . . yes . . . there."

The constable quickly gave directions to the banker's home, then told Longarm, "You go ahead with the ladies. I can take care of everything here. Chief Timmons will likely want to see you later to get a written report on what happened, but you can do that after you know the ladies are safe." Gilmore was speaking to Longarm but his eyes were on Glenda who had gotten up off the street and was busy brushing herself off.

"Timmons?" Longarm asked. "I don't know anybody by that name."

"The chief is new here," Gilmore said. "He's all right, though. You'll like him."

"I'm sure I will. For the meantime, though, I'll be with the ladies at this banker's house."

"Yes, sir." Gilmore smiled and shrugged. "Sorry for your welcome to our fair city. It ain't usually like this." This time he was definitely speaking to Glenda Palmer.

Longarm tossed his carpetbag onto the hand cart to be brought along later and took each female by the elbow to move them along. He really wanted to get them off the street now and inside where they should be safe from harm.

Chapter 10

"You were . . . were really quite magnificent," Mrs. Palmer gushed. "We could have been killed. We *would* have been killed. Oh, dear. This is terrible. To think . . . I never really believed it, you know. I thought it just so much silliness. But that man, that horrid horrid man . . ."

Longarm got the woman settled on a sofa, pulled a hassock near so she could get her feet up and went to the sideboard to pour a stout dollop of the banker's brandy into a snifter.

"Oh, no. Please. I couldn't."

"It's medicinal," he said. "Drink it."

"Yes, all right. If you say so." The lady tossed it back like a saloon floor regular. She did not make a face at the taste or the impact and her eyes did not water, so he poured her another and she drank that down, too.

The banker's wife, a small woman who looked like she was in her sixties or so but was still spry and lively, returned to the parlor from taking Glenda upstairs to recuperate from the ordeal of being shot at and then seeing the assailant gunned down in return.

Longarm could understand the girl being upset. Obvi-

51

ously, her life had been one of sheltered privilege. Right up until now.

"Is she all right?" Mrs. Belton asked, inquiring about Elspeth Palmer.

"Yes 'm, I'd say so. She will be anyway. While you were seeing to Glenda I made myself free with your brandy. I hope you don't mind."

"Not at all. Would you like another, dear?"

"Yes, please," Mrs. Palmer said, holding her glass out. Longarm hurried to take it to fill again.

Mrs. Belton dropped into one of the leather-covered wing chairs nearby but before she could get her skirts properly arranged there was the melodic chime of a ringing bell in the foyer. The lady of the house did not move. But then what was house help for if not to tend to the little things like responding to a doorbell.

"Ma'am," the uniformed maid said when she came into the parlor a few moments later. The woman—Mexican, Longarm thought—curtsied and bobbed her head.

"What is it, Maria?"

"There is a gentleman at the door, ma'am. A Constable Gilmore. He wants to see the Mr. Marshal."

"That'd be me," Longarm said, quickly standing. "If you would excuse me . . . ?"

"Yes, of course."

Longarm looked at Mrs. Palmer. She was halfway through this latest brandy and had some color back in her cheeks now. She had looked kind of peaked there for a little while. "I won't be long," he assured her, "and I won't be leaving you. I'll be right outside on the porch there."

"I shall see to her needs, deputy," the banker's lady assured him.

Longarm followed the maid out to the vestibule where

52

Gilmore was waiting. "Let's go outside, Jason. I'm dyin' for a smoke."

Gilmore smiled and pushed the door open, Longarm gratefully following.

"What's up?" Longarm asked once they were outdoors. He was already fishing inside his coat pocket for a cheroot. "Want a smoke?"

"No, thanks."

Longarm bit the twist off the tip of the slender cigar and quickly scratched a lucifer aflame so he could light it.

"I thought you'd want to know about that asshole who took a shot at you," Gilmore said, then frowned and quickly looked to make sure the front windows on the Belton house were closed against dust from the road. It would not do for strong language to make its way inside where the ladies could hear. A man like Belton could raise hell with City Hall, maybe even get Gilmore fired.

"What'd you find out?" Longarm asked.

"Let's go over here and set down. My feet are tired."

"You been running around that much with this thing?"

"No, but these boots are new. Do you mind?"

The two men sat on a pair of high-backed wicker chairs that were arranged on the front porch and Gilmore stuck his legs out in front of him, taking the weight off his feet. "There. That's better."

"Now what is it you know about that guy that shot at Miz Palmer?" Longarm asked.

Gilmore smiled a little. "I know . . . no, that isn't right . . . I don't actually *know* and never will. But I am fairly sure that the idiot was not shooting at either one of those women."

"I don't understand."

"Ever hear of a guy named Abner Leroy Wilkerson? Went by the name of Ab or sometimes Willie?"

Longarm shook his head. "No, not that I recall."

"Well, he knew about you. Recognized you, too," the local lawman said.

"Wilkerson," Longarm repeated. He turned the name over in his mind for a few moments but he was already sure. He had never heard of the son of a bitch before this moment. "No," he said firmly. "Rings no bells with me, Jason."

"Well, apparently, there was paper out on him. Or some damn thing. Ab Wilkerson punched cows for a man named Lew Thomas. Him and another hand had come in today to pick up some supplies. They stopped in to have a few drinks after their wagon was loaded. According to the fellow that was with him, Ab Wilkerson and this other gent had had their snort and were on their way back outside when Wilkerson seen you. He stopped short and . . . again it's according to this other fella . . . he said, 'Jesus Christ, it's that bastard Marshal Long. He's here after me, Billy. He's after me.' Then Wilkerson hauled out his iron, took careful aim, and you know the rest of it."

"What about the fellow who told you all this?"

"His name is Billy Hanlon. I've known him for years. He's a good cowhand, never a troublemaker, doesn't even wear a gun most of the time. Didn't have one on him today, as a matter of fact."

"Hanlon, Wilkerson," Longarm thought some more, then sighed. "No, I don't know either of them. Don't know of any paper out on them either."

"Anyway," Gilmore said, "it looks for sure like Wilkerson thought you were here for him. That's why he shot at you. He had no intention of hitting either one of those ladies."

"I'll be damned," Longarm mused. After a moment he grinned and said, "Do me a favor, Jason?"

"If I can, sure."

"Don't tell this to the Palmer ladies nor for the time bein' to the Beltons neither."

"All right, but why?"

"I've been having a helluva lot of trouble tryin' to get them two females to take the threats serious. Maybe now that they've been shot at . . . or anyhow think that they've been shot at . . . maybe they'll be more careful about wanderin' off the reservation. So to speak."

The Cheyenne constable chuckled. "You have my word on it, Longarm. I won't peach, not until you and those ladies are well gone out of here."

"You're a pal, Jason. Thanks." Longarm stood. He took another deep, slow drag on his cheroot—he hadn't yet smoked it halfway down—then reluctantly flicked it out into the banker's front yard. "Sure wish those women weren't so dead set against smoking," he said. "Is there anything else you need from me about this? Reports to sign or anything?"

"Thanks, but I can handle it. I just thought you ought to know what was going on."

Longarm grinned. "I owe you one, Jason."

The two lawmen shook hands, and Longarm went back inside the banker's mansion, Longarm marveling as he did so. Why, the Persian rugs in there were so thick a man couldn't hardly hear his boot heels on the floor when he walked across them, and the furnishings were both elegant and obviously expensive.

This was how the other half lived, he thought, as he returned to the parlor.

Chapter 11

Longarm lay in bed half awake, his belly warm and full with succulent beef roast and a superb bourbon. He didn't normally care all that much for bourbon but this private label was worth making an exception for Custis Long had damn little in common with the gray and balding banker who was his host for the night, but he surely did approve of the man's taste in whiskey. Cigars, too, for that matter.

Now he could relax. The Palmer women were safely secured for the night in two of the dozen or so guest bedrooms in the mansion, and Longarm's duty could be laid aside until daybreak.

He yawned, stretched, rolled onto his back and reached behind to plump the pillow under his neck; damn thing was a limp and skimpy feather pillow and needed some bulk in order to do him some good. The sheets were cool and smooth, not at all like the rough flannel he was accustomed to sleeping in.

A man could get used to all this luxury, he thought. And like it.

He felt himself drifting lightly into sleep.

Then came wide awake to the creak of a footstep and the faint squeal of a protesting hinge.

A wedge of pale lamplight from the hallway briefly illuminated the foot of his bed then quickly disappeared as the door was eased shut.

In the darkness that followed, Longarm's hand sought the familiar butt of his Colt dangling on the bedpost. He eased the gun out of its holster and drew it beneath the covers with him.

There was no light to really see by but he could dimly make out a pale ghost-shape at the foot of the bed. Formless. Floating.

Except, dammit, there are no ghosts. Longarm knew that.

And if there were ghosts they would not mutter when they bumped into the bed.

They would not cause the mattress to tilt when they put their weight on the side of the bed, and they would not pull the covers away from Longarm's chest when they crawled in with him.

Most assuredly a ghost would not find and fondle his cock underneath those covers.

Longarm smiled as he silently returned the Colt to its place and reached down.

He encountered a nest of soft, tousled hair. A smooth cheek. An eager mouth.

His nocturnal visitor felt his searching hand and lightly took hold of it, turning it and taking his thumb into her mouth. She sucked his thumb deep, then let it slide away, the moisture giving an impression of cold when it hit the air and began to evaporate.

He felt her head dip and a moment later she pulled his partially erect cock into her mouth.

"Why don't you . . ." he began.

"Shh!" she quickly cut him off. "Shh."

She returned to what she was doing, tonguing the length of his cock and slowly, thoroughly licking his balls before again pulling him inside her mouth.

Longarm hadn't realized just how horny he was after some days without getting it off. He felt the rise of that sweet sap almost immediately and thrust his hips upward, forcing himself deep into her mouth while he spewed jism into her throat.

She gagged and squirmed for a moment in obvious discomfort, then resumed sucking only long enough to satisfy herself that he remained hard.

She rose up, the bedcovers draped over her and hiding her completely, and turned around so that she was straddling him with her knees, facing away toward his feet, her back to him.

His eyes had adjusted as much as was possible, but even so he could see nothing more than a pale shape that was her nightgown and a dark spill of hair falling almost to her waist.

She lifted herself up and took his cock in one hand to guide him into the hot, slippery depths of her body.

When she lowered herself onto him, Longarm could hear a very faint whimper although whether of pain at having to accommodate his length or pleasure because of his large size he could not guess.

She sat up and brushed her hair back, lifting it with both hands and fluffing it out before letting it fall onto her shoulders and back. Then she gave her attention to the business at hand, pumping gently at first. Then faster. And finally bucking and thrusting like a wild thing, like a machine run amok.

Longarm could feel her frantic gyrations and hear her breath rasping between clenched teeth. She began to emit a low, keening noise and then . . . then she reached climax.

She cried out and her vaginal lips clenched and spasmed around his shaft as the sensations threatened to overwhelm her.

The lady's climax was what he had been waiting for, and again Longarm spat the juices of his lust. The release was powerful, and he collapsed. Until that moment he really hadn't realized how tightly strung his body was.

Now it was like cutting the strings of a marionette. He sank back, utterly spent, intending to rest there for just a minute or two before pulling her up to cuddle against his shoulder while both of them recuperated from the powerful climax they had shared.

He never got the chance to do that, however.

The woman lifted herself off him and slid out from under the covers.

He could hear her progress as she padded barefoot across the floor.

All he could see was that pale shape, as insubstantial as a wisp of cloud.

Light from the doorway briefly flared and then again was gone as she slipped out into the hallway without Longarm ever getting a good look at her.

It occurred to him only later, when he was once more drifting down toward slumber, that he really did not know who the hell it was who had come to him. Mrs. Elspeth Palmer. Glenda Palmer. Or, hell, the banker's wife. One of the maids.

It could have been any one of them.

Whoever it was, Longarm wore a satisfied smile when he dropped into a deep and restful sleep.

Chapter 12

Tea. What the hell was it about anything as weak and useless as tea that made these women so attracted to it. No whiskey. No beer. Not even coffee, for Pete's sake. Tea.

And little bitty finger sandwiches with the crusts cut off. Egg salad. Watercress . . . watercress! Really. In a sandwich. A man might as well go out on the range and take to eating grass alongside the cows as try to get along on the grub these hoity-toity damn women served at their suffragette meetings.

There was not a single damn thing that a fellow could sink his teeth into.

Well, other than a very few of the women themselves. The general run of the herd, he was finding, were old, wrinkled and sour. But here and there among them you could find a pert and pretty little filly who was worth a second look.

So Longarm sat. His belly rumbling for lack of something substantial to put into it. And admired those few ladies who were worth looking at. Glenda Palmer, for instance.

Today, he was happy to discover, the girl was not so anxious to slip away on her own. And judging by the way both mother and daughter acted toward him they were finally taking the death threats seriously. Why, they weren't even surly or dismissive toward him. Sometimes Longarm almost thought they remembered he was there.

He found a place for himself close to the buffet spread, settled back and tried to make the best of a bad deal.

The suffragette luncheon was being held in the banker's house. It was attended by fourteen females and was not open to the public.

When the salad forks had all been laid aside and the meeting portion of things was about to get started, Mrs. Palmer approached Longarm. He stood. "Yes, ma'am?"

"You look bored, deputy."

He did not try to deny it. Hell, he *was* bored. Who the devil wouldn't be?

"We will be talking here all afternoon. No one else will be admitted and everyone here is well known to our hostess. It shouldn't be necessary for you to sit through all of this. It would be sensible, I think, for you to have some free time to, oh, do whatever it is you men do when you are on your own in a strange town. Why don't you go about your own affairs for the afternoon? Glenda and I are quite safe here, and neither one of us will be going anywhere until tomorrow morning. You should consider yourself free until suppertime or thereabouts. How does that sound?"

Longarm reached for his hat. "That's mighty thoughtful of you, Miz Palmer. Thanks."

"We shall see you this evening then, deputy."

Longarm glanced back at Glenda. He suspected hers was the firm, eager body that had pleased him in the night. She acted just a little suspiciously, carefully avoiding looking in his direction, tensing up just a little bit when he was near.

Not a bad-looking girl, Glenda. He hoped she would want to come back for seconds tonight.

In the meantime . . . "I'll see you this evening then, Miz Palmer."

He got the hell out of there.

Duty was duty and a job was a job, but sometimes a fellow just wants to lay back and enjoy life. That is what Custis Long was doing at that moment.

He was seated at a baize-covered table in the Hungry Dog saloon with four friendly strangers, a fan of cards in his hand and half a glass of rye whiskey warming his belly, the other half on the table beside him. A slender cheroot smoldered in a tin ashtray by his elbow.

"Dealer takes two," a gent in shirtsleeves and a string tie declared before discarding a pair of pasteboards and sliding their replacements off the top of the deck. "Anybody open?"

"I'll open for ten cents."

"I'm in," the fellow to Longarm's right said, tossing two nickels into the pot.

Longarm looked at his cards dispassionately. All he had was king high to nothing and there was no likelihood of this hand going anywhere with a crap hand like that. Not that he really minded. The play was low-stakes and honest, conducted for pleasure more than profit.

"Fold," he said, closing the fan into a thin sheaf of cards and tossing them down.

He took a deep swallow of the rye and a pull on the cheroot and sat back to observe the others.

Movement at the batwings caught his attention, and he smiled when he saw Constable Gilmore come in.

Longarm's smile died when Gilmore spotted him and hurried across the room to the table.

"I've been looking everywhere for you, marshal," he said, chest heaving for breath.

"Is there a problem, Jason?"

"I'll say. That blond girl Glenda? She's missing. Kidnapped it looks like."

"Oh, shit." Longarm came to his feet, the card game and half-finished drink forgotten. "How? When? Is there a ransom demand or a note or . . . hell, or anything?"

Gilmore shook his head. "She's just missing."

"She was supposed to stay there at Belton's house."

"Yes, and my little brother is supposed to keep his mouth closed when he's in Sunday school but that doesn't mean that he does it. Anyway I don't know what's happened. You . . . you'll just have to talk to the mother, that's all."

"Excuse me, gents," Longarm said to the fellows at the table. He jammed the cheroot between his teeth and headed for the banker's place.

Chapter 13

The Belton house was filled with tears and recrimination. The suffragettes were gone, and Elspeth Palmer and Idamae Belton were in the parlor wringing their hands and bawling, each of them yammering aloud that she and she alone was responsible—somehow—for the kidnapping. Neither got around to saying just exactly *how* she was responsible though.

There was a helluva lot of "I could have" and "I should have" going around. Longarm contributed his own thoughts in that vein, although he did not bother to speak them aloud.

He could have stopped the kidnapping had he remained at his post, here at the house, instead of accepting Mrs. Palmer's offer of some time off.

He should have tended to business. It was something Billy Vail was bound to mention.

Mention? Billy was very likely going to ream Longarm a new asshole over this.

Oh, the boss wouldn't show it all that much. He would not scream and shout and slam around the office. That was not his style. And if the truth were known, Custis Long

65

would rather see Billy throw a screaming fit than endure his cold and stony looks of disappointment.

Billy was perfectly capable of clouding up and raining all over a man. That was one thing. But it was far worse when he turned to stone. Then a deputy knew that things were damn-all serious.

And this one would be.

Unless Longarm could ease some of the sting by getting that girl back unharmed. Quickly.

He knelt in front of a nearly hysterical Elspeth Palmer and took hold of her hand, the one that was not clutching a sopping wet handkerchief. "Ma'am? Miz Palmer? Tell me what happened. Please. I need t' know so's I can find Glenda an' get her back here to you."

Mrs. Palmer's shoulders shook. She wailed aloud. Tears ran down her cheeks and snot streamed over her upper lip. She kept dabbing at both the tears and the snot.

"Mrs. Palmer? Please."

"I can tell you what little we know, deputy," Idamae Belton put in, having to raise her voice to be heard above Elspeth Palmer's anguished cries.

"Please."

Mrs. Belton nodded to him, then motioned her maid nearer. "Maria. Take care of Elspeth, please. Take her upstairs and put her to bed, then have Martha make her some comfrey tea. And put a little laudanum in her tea. That will help her sleep."

"Yes 'm."

Mrs. Belton stood and motioned for Longarm to follow. She led him into the next room, still full of tables set with the remains of the ladies' luncheon. Jason Gilmore tagged along behind. The room, like the emotions of the women who had been here, was in disarray. That would be easy

66

enough to tidy up when someone got around to it. Longarm was not so sure how simple it would be to get things back to normal should any harm come to Glenda however.

"Sit down, gentlemen, please. Would you like tea? Coffee?"

"What we'll be needin', ma'am, is information. As much as we can get an' as quick as we can get it. Now, tell us everything you can think of from the time I left the room on. Even if you think somethin' is completely unimportant, tell us anyway. Ya never know what might turn out t' be important, so the more we know the better it will be."

"Very well." Mrs. Belton paused for a moment and took a deep breath. Then she began to speak, reaching into her memory for everything she could recall.

Chapter 14

The two lawmen stepped out onto the front porch. Longarm pulled a pair of cheroots from his inside coat pocket and offered one to Gilmore, who shook his head so Longarm returned the cigar to his pocket.

"Seems simple enough, don't it," Longarm said, going about the busywork of trimming and lighting the cheroot.

Jason nodded. "There isn't a thing that could've been done differently even if you'd been sitting right there in that room," he said.

"If I had been there. . . ." Longarm began.

"Oh, bullshit. If you'd been there, there wouldn't have been a thing different. The girl had to take a piss. Now tell me the truth. She was in friendly surroundings. Nobody but a bunch of crazy damn women around. And she had to go take a piss. Are you gonna stand there and seriously tell me that you woulda gone to the bathroom with her?"

"Well, maybe I . . ."

"*Maybe* my hairy pink ass," Gilmore snapped. "You would've sat right there and had another piece of pie."

"They weren't serving pie," Longarm protested. "It was some sort of strawberry compote."

"Don't quibble. You would have sat right there. The girl would have gone off to take her leak. And whatever happened would have gone right ahead and happened anyway."

Longarm grunted and crossed his arms, smoking in sullen silence. He did not, however, try to dispute Jason Gilmore's reasoning. The young deputy could well be right in what he said, even if he was just trying to make Longarm feel better about this.

After a moment, Longarm exhaled a stream of aromatic smoke, then said, "How'd he know?"

"What?"

"The kidnapper. How'd he know when he could snatch Glenda? How'd he know where to lie in wait for her?"

"Could be he was wanting to grab the first of those women who came along," Gilmore suggested.

"That would mean the Palmer women weren't the ones targeted, that Glenda was taken by chance." He shook his head. "I can't buy that. Coincidence has no place in a crime investigation."

"Coincidences happen."

"Yeah, but I don't believe in the son o' bitches. No, I have t' figure Glenda was the target. Her or her mama. Putting pressure on Howard Palmer is the whole reason for all this."

"It could have nothing to do with the congressman," Jason argued. "They are here raising hell about women's voting rights. It could be someone who opposes that."

"Who? Wyoming already gives women the right to vote," Longarm said.

"Only in local and territorial matters. The women here have got a taste of what it means to vote. They want more. Them and their kind want women to have full voting rights all over the country."

70

"Believe me, I know that. I've been forced to listen to their claptrap for the past couple days. Some of these suffragettes are militant as hell. I wouldn't be surprised at much of anything from the likes o' them."

"So it's reasonable to assume that the men who hold an opposite view could be just as stubborn," Gilmore said. "Some of them could have taken Glenda to make some sort of stupid point or to get her mother to quit campaigning, something like that."

Longarm took another drag on his cheroot and shook his head. "I still think this would've been different if I'd been in there where I was s'posed t' be."

"Quit feeling sorry for yourself and pay attention to business," Gilmore snapped.

Longarm sighed. "I reckon I am, ain't I?"

"Yes, I reckon you are. Now let's you and me get down to cases on this. I think we can agree that the kidnapping is aimed at her father. One way or the other, whether it's trying to get him to support voting rights for women or because of this crazy idea that red Indians should have sovereign land rights, whoever took that girl wants to influence her father's votes in congress."

"Yep. Only reason I can think of." Longarm scratched his chin and glanced over his shoulder to make sure no one from the Belton household was within earshot. "Either that or because she's a fine looking piece of ass an' somebody wants t' cut a piece o' that for hisself."

"She does look good enough to eat, doesn't she?"

"Are the fellas around here so hard up for pussy that they'd kidnap a congressman's daughter?"

"Not likely," Jason said. "Women are cheap and most of them are easy. A fella shouldn't have to steal it." Gilmore frowned and thought for a moment, then said, "Somebody with a real yen for a virgin maybe?"

"If the girl *is* a virgin," Longarm said, thinking about the previous night and his mysterious visitor.

"Whether she is or not, she sure as hell looks like a virgin. She looks like butter wouldn't melt in her mouth. Or anywhere else."

"This isn't getting us nowhere."

"No," Gilmore agreed. "It isn't. Did you see any men in or around the house today?"

"Just me and the banker an' he left early t' go to the bank. I gather he don't come home for lunch or anyway wasn't goin' to with all them suffragettes underfoot. Come to think of it, does it have t' be a man that done the kidnapping?"

"Why would a woman want to snatch her?"

"Shit, I dunno. Some woman whose husband hold grazing rights on one of the Indian reservations or one whose hubby has some mineral located on Indian land and doesn't want to get shut out? Congressman Palmer's bill would play hob with an awful lot of Wyoming ranchers an' miners," Longarm said. "It could be anyone connected with any one of them. Even their women an' never mind the voting thing."

"In other words, you're saying the girl could have been taken by almost anyone."

"That's about the size of it," Longarm agreed. "Unfortunately."

"We need to find her, Long. We need to do it before anything happens to her."

"I agree. Tell me where she is an' I'll go fetch her back to mama."

They stood there in silence for a few moments longer

while Longarm finished his cheroot, then walked around to the back of the house to see if there were any telltale footprints or other helpful evidence that might point them toward the missing girl.

Chapter 15

"Shit," Longarm grumbled. "There's nothing but scuff marks."

"Even if there had been footprints," Jason said, "they would have been rubbed out by now. I saw Ned Baines heading into the alley a little while ago."

"Who's he? A suspect maybe?"

"Not a chance. Ned drives the coal wagon. He makes deliveries for Truman Johnston. Ned is a Saturday night drunk and a Sunday morning deacon. He's as honest as the day is long. And before you ask, the fellow he works for, Truman, owns Wyoming Coal and Salt. The company has a warehouse over by the train tracks. Truman supplies probably every house and business in and around Cheyenne with coal and nearly every ranch in eastern Wyoming and western Nebraska with salt for their range cattle."

"Could he be a suspect?"

"Marshal, I'd think almost any man or woman around here could be a suspect one way or another, but Truman?" Gilmore shook his head. "Not likely. He's a fence-sitter. Truman has contracts with the territorial government and he wants to keep them regardless of which party is in office at any given moment. I can't imagine him taking a firm position on anything for fear he might offend one group or another. That would include women. Don't forget, the ladies already have the vote here for local and county elections."

"That works out all right, does it?"

"Better than you might think," Gilmore said. "Of course most women vote however their husbands tell them to." He grinned and added, "Or so the husbands think. Once they get inside that booth and pull the curtain, who's to know how they really vote."

"The threat against the Palmers is supposed to come from the cattlemen and the mining interests," Longarm said. "From the big money boys. Any one of them or maybe a group of them acting together could afford to hire someone to kidnap the congressman's daughter. It wouldn't have to be someone with an ax to grind his own self. Could as likely be someone who's doing it strictly for the cash."

"If that is the case," Jason said, "they would surely keep her alive."

Longarm nodded. "Likely. Unless this jasper realizes that the girl is more of a threat to him alive than she would be dead. Wouldn't be the first time someone's tried to ransom a body that doesn't happen t' be breathing no more."

"Have you ever dealt with a kidnapping before?"

"Sad to say, Jason, yes, I have."

"This is my first," the young deputy admitted.

"Give me a straightforward robber or murderer any-time," Longarm said. "Kidnappers an' rapists an' like that are the ones that make my skin crawl. It ain't money with them nor anger; they got no feeling for folks. They violate people. That's what pisses me off about 'em."

"I never thought of it like that."

"These kidnaps you've been in or before. Did you get the victims back alive?"

Longarm hesitated, then in a soft, sad voice said, "Most o' the time, Jason. Only most o' the time."

"Sorry."

"Failure cuts deep, I reckon." The tall deputy squared his shoulders and in a crisp tone of voice said, "Point is, Jason, you and me got our work cut out for us here. We need t' find that girl an' the quicker we do that the better."

"So we're looking for pretty much any man, woman or child in Cheyenne or maybe in the whole of Wyoming Territory."

"Hell, we can drop the children as suspects. That trims the list of possible suspects down some. See there? We're already making progress with this thing," Longarm said with a grin. "A couple minutes thinking and we've already cut out a third of the herd."

"Sounds almost easy when you put it that way."

"Now let's us go look for a live and sassy Miss Palmer 'cause getting her back is our first concern here. Finding out who's behind the kidnapping can come after."

Chapter 16

"No, sir, I never seen nothing like that. Nothing a'tall. Sorry that I can't he'p you. I surely would if'n I could."

"All right. Thank you, ma'am," Longarm said. He made a half bow toward the wrinkled and worn-out little woman and turned away from her door while setting his Stetson back onto his head.

He, Jason Gilmore and two other Cheyenne constables were engaged in walking the streets and the alleys in a three-block radius around the Belton mansion, asking everyone they could find if they had seen anything suspicious.

So far Longarm had been able to come up with exactly nothing. No young girl struggling or in any way looking as if she were in distress. No enclosed carriages or coaches that could hide Glenda and her kidnappers. No wagons with closed containers of any sort large enough to hold a girl of Glenda's size. No . . . no anything remotely suspicious. Dammit!

Wearily, he walked on to the next place and let himself in at the gate. The house was small, with a covered porch along the front and one side. Climbing plants with trumpet-shaped blossoms on them grew profusely on thin slats that almost enclosed the porch into another room, at least insofar as privacy was concerned.

When Longarm mounted the steps onto the porch he discovered an elderly man sitting in a rocking chair behind the screen of greenery. A three-point trade blanket lay over his lap, covering his legs, and a heavy knitted shawl was draped across his shoulders. His hands were tucked under the blanket.

He was a small and shrunken figure sitting there, white hair unkempt beneath a ratty badger fur hat and a close-trimmed white beard showing yellow tobacco stains beneath both corners of his mouth. He looked like he was ready for burial except for a pair of startling bright blue eyes that were wide open and fixed upon Longarm.

"Looking for somebody, are you?"

"Why would you think that?"

"Seen you all up and down this street. You and a young fella I recognize to be a town deputy."

"The constable and a few others are helping me," Longarm said, "and yes, we're lookin' for somebody."

"Would that make you a police officer, mister?" the old man asked.

"Deputy U.S. marshal, actually." Longarm introduced himself.

"Long. Custis Long," the old man mused aloud, taking one hand out from under the blanket and scratching beside his nose. After a moment he nodded. "Oh, yes. You and another federal boy took down that bunch of train robbers over by Evanston a year or two back."

"That's right. Me an' a deputy called Smiley. How'd you know that?"

The old man cackled, his bony shoulders rising and falling. "I may be old, sonny, but I still got all my thinking faculties. The body is giving up but the mind is not. My name is Tom Harmon, and I used to be a railroad detective. I still have some friends on the line. They come by now and then. We talk. It helps me to keep up with things. Has there been another train robbery?"

"No, sir. Kidnapping this time."

"In broad daylight?"

"Yes, sir." Longarm told him about Glenda's disappearance.

"I know the place, of course. What little banking I do is with Belton. Before my wife died, while I could still get around some, we were invited to the Beltons' Christmas soiree every year. Who did you say this girl is?"

Longarm told him.

"Oh, yes. That idiot. I've read what the newspapers have to say about her daddy, and I have to agree with the cattlemen about the congressman's proposals. Abandoning sovereignty over those lands would be sheer lunacy. It would set a very bad precedent and take away all our options for the future. And for no purpose other than to make Congressman Palmer the subject of conversation. Mark my words, young man." The old fellow waggled a bony finger at Longarm. "Palmer intends making a run for the Whig presidential nomination."

"Could be," Longarm conceded.

Harmon snorted. " 'Could be, my ass. Count on it. 'Tis as certain as sunrise."

"Yes, sir," Longarm said politely. It did not matter if he agreed with the comment or did not, he was not going to dispute it.

"Now the daughter has been kidnapped, you say?"

"Yes, sir. From the house. In broad daylight."

"So you would be looking for a coach, a carriage, a

deep-sided dray or any sort of wagon carrying a large crate, something big enough to hide the girl and probably covered over with quilts or buffalo robes, something like that to muffle any sounds she might make like shouting for help or kicking her feet."

"Yes, sir, exactly." Longarm was more than a little surprised by the old fellow's immediate grasp of what he was looking for. But then Harmon said he had been a railroad detective. He understood.

"I've been sitting here since not long after sunup, deputy."

"Longarm," Longarm corrected. "My friends call me Longarm. I'd be pleased if you was t' do that, too."

"All right, son. You can call me *Mr.* Harmon."

Longarm's expression must have registered his surprise because seconds after he said that Harmon broke into laughter. "I didn't mean that, Longarm. Call me Tom, please."

Longarm grinned. "Yes, sir."

"Tom," Harmon said.

"Right. Tom."

"Anyway, as I was saying before you interrupted me, I've been sitting right here most of the day. I won't pretend to remember everyone who has gone by but most of them have been townsfolk either riding saddle horses or on foot. As for driven rigs, the usual milk wagon went by early. And Belton's light rig went toward his house about lunchtime and back again a half hour or so later. The top was down though and I can tell you there was no kidnapped girl riding in it when he went back to the bank after dinner." He paused to scratch again. "Then there was the coal wagon . . ."

"Ned Baines making deliveries," Longarm said. "We already know about him."

Harmon nodded. "And Marvin Hollander's dray. That was a mite strange since this is not one of his normal delivery days. Usually he makes his deliveries on Mondays, Wednesdays and Fridays."

"Hollander, you say? Who would he be?" Longarm asked.

"Deals in hardware," Harmon said.

"Close to the cattlemen, would you say?"

"Son, we almost all of us here are close to the cattlemen, one way or another. Even those of us who are . . . or were . . . associated with the railroad are in bed with the beef interests. Don't forget, money begets money. And money's best friend is money. You have to understand that if you hope to understand business."

"So you are saying . . ." Longarm prompted.

"I am saying that I haven't seen a thing today that would be of any help to you in your search for the girl, but I am also saying that you should not take anyone or anything at face value. People will do the goddamnedest things when their flow of money is at stake. And the more money is involved the crazier they can get." Harmon laughed. "It is a whole lot easier for a poor man to be honest than it is for the rich. The Bible says that, you know."

"It does?"

"Not in so many words, but yes. It does."

Longarm sighed. "Thank you for your help, Mister . . ." He paused and grinned, then corrected his error. "Thanks for your help, Tom."

"I've been no help at all. But I am sure you have sense

enough to go check on what Marvin Hollander's dray was up to today. I can also assure you that if I hear anything that will help, I will get word to you about it." The old fellow cackled. "I see and hear more than you might think, and I am not quite so helpless as I like folks to believe." Harmon turned down the top of his lap robe to display a pair of engraved Colt revolvers lying there atop his withered thighs.

The Colts were the antiquated cap and ball models, .36 Navy arms on the 1861 pattern, Longarm saw, not only deadly weapons but probably the prettiest pistols ever designed. These showed wear and use but appeared to be immaculately clean and oiled. Anyone who tried to give the old man trouble was going to find himself with more than he expected and probably more than he could handle. Longarm liked old Tom Harmon. He surely did.

"Thank you, sir."

"You are quite welcome, young man. Good luck."

Chapter 17

"I see you met our senior statesman," Jason Gilmore said, falling into step with Longarm on the street.

"Old Tom? Yes. I like him."

"So do I. The chief of police hates him."

Longarm raised an eyebrow.

"Tom has been known to show him up. In public. At the town council meetings."

Longarm chuckled. "Fortunately it ain't my ox been gored so I got no quarrel with the man. Are we about done on this block?"

The local constable nodded. "I already sent Mader and Whistler over to the next street to start over there." Ben Mader and the constable called Whistler—Longarm had no idea if that was the man's name or simply a nickname— were the two other men Gilmore had enlisted in the search for Glenda and her kidnappers. Gilmore, Mader and Whistler constituted the entire police force available in Cheyenne at the moment. But then this crime had occurred at the banker's home, and William Belton was a man of considerable influence in the town. Longarm found it not at all surprising that the city would do everything possible to help find Glenda Palmer and effect her rescue.

"I figure you and I can take this block over here," Gilmore said as they rounded the street corner. "You take whichever side you want. I'll take the other."

"Fine by me, I'll . . ."

Longarm was interrupted by the sounds of gunfire and breaking glass coming from somewhere ahead and to their left.

Both he and Jason broke into a run, guns drawn, heading toward the source of those shots.

"Aw, shit!" Jason groaned when they reached the next corner.

Ben Mader was crouching behind a water trough, his revolver aimed in the direction of a tidy little house set just off the street with hollyhocks growing in the front yard.

A puff of white smoke appeared at the right front window and another gunshot boomed out. Longarm could hear the dull thump of the bullet striking the side of the trough where Mader was taking cover.

The constable fired back but even from the end of the block Longarm could see that the officer just snapped his shot in the general direction of the house without taking aim.

"Where is Sam?" Gilmore asked, worry lying heavy in his voice.

Longarm assumed Sam would be the man who had been introduced to him as Whistler.

"Quick," Longarm said, "go around back. Make sure they don't try to slip out that way. I want t' go see that your boy Mader don't put a bullet in the Palmer girl accidental-like. He's firing blind an' not thinking that bullets can pass through walls an' doors an' windows an'

86

such. If that girl is in there he could kill her instead o' one of those kidnappers."

"All right. I'll go through the alley and watch for them to make a break," Gilmore responded. Neither he nor Longarm seemed to so much as notice that the federal officer was taking charge here. Longarm was older and more experienced, and they could sort out any questions of jurisdiction afterward.

Another shot was fired, this one from the other of the two front windows. Shards of broken glass blew out, some flying all the way to the street. The door, Longarm noted, was closed. Constable Mader stayed in his crouch, hiding low behind the heavy planks of the water trough, but he waved his revolver in the direction of the house and loosed off another round of return fire. God knew where that bullet went. Longarm guessed Mader hadn't even hit the house with it.

"Quit that, dammit," Longarm shouted as he stretched his legs into a dash along the macadamized city street.

"Is that you, Marshal? Whadda you want?"

Longarm reached Mader and knelt beside the man, his upper body fully exposed above the level of the trough, his eyes trained on those two windows at the front of the house even when he spoke to the constable.

"You ain't gonna do any good down there on your belly, son. You got no idea where them bullets is going. Aimed fire, lad. The only way you can hit anything is t' take your time an' draw a fine bead."

"But if I sit up they can shoot me," Mader protested.

"Yeah, well, that's why the city pays you so damn much," Longarm said with a grin, glancing down at the young constable for a moment.

Mader was pale and shaking. "I've never been shot at before." His tone was apologetic.

"Just remember that the other guy is as scared as you are, Ben. An' you are the one in the right."

"Jesus!" Mader blurted.

Longarm's grin got wider. "It don't hurt none to pray. Just keep your eyes open while you're doin' it. You don't want a stray slug hitting that girl, do you? You'd feel awful bad about that. Now sit up an' look where you're shooting."

Mader came onto his knees.

White gunsmoke blossomed at both front windows at almost the same moment. One bullet found the side of the trough again. Longarm heard the other sizzle overhead and a window on the house across the street break.

Longarm fired quickly, sending a round through the right-hand window. Young constable Ben Mader hesitated for a moment, then aimed and fired at the left-hand window.

"That's better," Longarm encouraged him. "Much better."

"What about the girl? Mightn't we hit her if we keep shooting?"

"Not if we're careful," Longarm said. "If they have her in the front room with them they'll likely have her pushed down on the floor. We're shooting from down here at the level o' the street, shooting just a little bit uphill so t' speak 'cause of the house being up off the ground some on them foundation pilings you see there. That means our angle o' fire will likely send our slugs high once they get past the windowsills. That's so long as we don't shoot wild an' send one into the wallboards down too low. D'you see what I mean?"

"Yes, sir. I think so."

"Good." Longarm held his Colt ready. "I'll cover both windows for a minute now an' you can reload."

"Re . . . ? Oh! I forgot."

"In a gunfight, son, you reload your piece every chance you get. It could save your life sometime if you remember t' do that." Longarm grinned again. "You just can't imagine how embarrassing it can be t' face somebody down if your gun is empty."

That elicited a smile from the constable, just the reaction Longarm was hoping for.

"All right, Marshal. I'm ready now if you want to reload."

Longarm nodded and flipped open the loading gate on his Colt. "You're gonna be fine, Ben. Just fine."

The young man grinned. But Longarm noticed he kept his eyes on the house while he did so. Ben Mader was learning fast.

But then in the business of law enforcement an officer either learned fast or died early. Those were often the choices.

Chapter 18

"Shouldn't you be staying lower than that, Marshal?"

"I can see better this way," Longarm said. He was exposed from his solar plexus upward, kneeling more or less in plain sight from the house windows. "It would take an aimed shot to hit me," he explained. "In order to take aim, they'd have t' show themselves. I got every confidence I could bust 'em before they could draw a good bead an' get an aimed shot off in this direction." He smiled. "They ain't firing as wild as you was a while ago but they ain't taking close aim neither."

"Do you even think they're still in there?" Mader asked. "We haven't seen nor heard anything of them in twenty, thirty minutes or so."

"They're still there. Jason is around back in the alley watching so they don't sneak off that way. I assume that's where the other constable . . . Sam, is it? I'm assuming that's where he is, too. Is that right?"

Ben Mader went pale. "He . . . I thought you knew. Whistler is dead. That's what started this fight."

"Dead? What happened?"

91

"He's laying in those bushes over there. They shot him, marshal. They gunned him down like a dog."

Longarm frowned. The fact that these kidnappers had already killed a lawman made things all the worse. They knew they would hang if they were taken alive. There was no threat anyone could hold over them to assure Glenda's safety. "Tell me about it, Ben."

"I don't know everything for sure. I was across the street. Working that side while Whistler was knocking on doors. I was too far away to overhear exactly what he said but what we been doing is we'd knock on the door, then announce ourselves when somebody opened up or if they just called out to see who it was. I was paying attention to the houses over on my own side of the street, you understand."

"Of course."

"So I never knew anything was different over here until I heard the first shot. I looked and . . . oh, Jesus! I never saw a man killed before today."

"It's all right, Ben. Take your time. Take a few deep breaths."

Mader gulped for air. He looked like he might puke at any moment but Longarm saw his throat working, likely swallowing back the impulse. "They hit Sam in the belly, it looked like. He doubled over and fell and rolled off the edge of the porch. He's laying right over there." The young constable pointed. "If you know just exactly where to look you can see a little patch of blue. That would be Sam's britches. Then after . . . after Sam went off the porch those sons of bitches in there shot some more. Wild shooting. Then one of them hollered something . . . I figure they must have looked out and seen me . . . and that's when they started shooting at me.

"I was halfway across the street, thinking to see could I

do anything to help Sam. Next thing I knew I was on my belly behind this here trough." He looked down at himself and made a wry face. "I just got this shirt back from the laundry, marshal. Now I've got mud all over it."

"Better mud from some horse's slobber than blood from a hole in your chest, kid."

"Yeah, I guess that'd be so."

"I'm sorry about your friend."

"Yes, sir."

"The good thing is that we know those guys didn't slip out the back way before Jason got around behind them."

"How do we know that, marshal?"

"Because they've been shooting at us after Jason would have had time to get back there."

"You think they're still there then?" Longarm was not sure but he thought the young constable sounded more than a little hopeful that the kidnappers would have made an escape and the house be empty now.

"I'm sure of it."

Mader sighed. Then he shifted uncomfortably.

"I have a job for you if you care to take it on. It could be dangerous but I know you can handle it," Longarm said.

"I . . . I'll try, sir."

"It's getting kinda hot an' I don't know about you but I'm getting thirsty."

"Me, too."

"There's something about bullets flying that increases the thirst. Damn if I know what would cause that but I know it t' be true. You can ask any lawman or soldier about that. Anyway, what I'd like for you t' do, Ben, is to go get something for us to drink. Something for Jason . . . you can take it through the alley and find him . . . give him his drink an' fill him in on where we are an' what we're up

93

to . . . then come back with somethin' for you an' me. A bucket o' beer, maybe."

"Beer! Wouldn't that . . . well, wouldn't that make us drunk?"

"I said one bucket for the two o' us, son, not a barrel. I dunno about you, but one bucket o' beer ain't gonna get me drunk. Now go on. I'll cover you in case somebody steps up t' one o' them windows."

"Yes, sir. I'll be quick as I can be."

"That's fine but don't worry about it. I ain't going anywhere as long as they don't. An' while you're doing that errand you might as well do another. You could find the mayor . . . the police chief is outta town, ain't he?"

"Yes, sir, he is."

"Then find the mayor. Tell him we're gonna need a couple dozen good lanterns with good wicks an' full reservoirs so they'll burn all night. Them and some real long poles that we can use to hang 'em on an' maneuver them closer to that house without us getting shot."

"Lanterns, sir?"

"If those men haven't give up by nightfall they'll be hoping to slip away in the dark. That's the way they'll be thinking. You can count on it. What I want t' do is to keep enough light on the place that they can't sneak out, with or without the girl. That's what I need the lanterns for."

"Who is going to place them close to the house, marshal?" It was obvious that that one was an errand young Ben Mader did not want to perform.

"That'd be my job," Longarm reassured him. "Now go on. I'm gettin' so dry I might could wither up an' blow away before you get back here with that beer."

"Yes, sir." The constable stuffed his revolver back into

its holster, braced himself and then launched himself into a head-down, elbows-flapping run down the street toward a clutch of interested onlookers who had gathered at the end of the block.

Chapter 19

"I wish there was some way t' make all them gawkers go the hell away," Longarm grumbled. Both ends of the city block were closed off, packed solid with men, women and what looked like every school-age kid in Cheyenne. The crowd was mostly quiet but there were always a few smart-asses in any group and this one was no exception. Those worthy citizens were whooping and catcalling and yelling their support to one side or the other, mostly to the kidnappers.

A preacher came and offered his services as a mediator.

"I can't tell you t' put your life on the line, padre," Longarm told him.

"And if I choose to speak with them without your authorization?" the gentleman asked.

"You're free, white an' twenty-one. That sorta thing would be entirely up t' you, your own self."

"Then I intend to bring peace to this community without any more bloodshed," the preacher declared in a voice loud enough to be heard inside the embattled house. "I shall offer those men in there safe conduct." He could certainly be heard inside the house. And for that matter, Longarm noted, he likely could be heard by the crowds at either end of the street, too. The preacher seemed to be angling for some public acclaim here. A little fame to boost his attendance at Sunday services? And the take in the collection basket, too?

Maybe. But then it could very well be that the man was sincere and thought that halting this gun battle was part of his mission on earth. "You do what you got t' do, preacher."

The gentleman—Longarm never had gotten his name—stood from behind the water trough, tugged down the tails of his coat and set his hat firmly on his head.

"You in there. Do not fire. I am coming to talk with you. There is no need for you to be afraid. I am not armed."

Clutching a worn Bible, the preacher marched forward. He unlatched the gate in the knee-high scantling fence that surrounded the yard and let himself in.

"I am coming in now."

The moment the preacher's shoe thumped on the wooden step leading onto the narrow porch there was a burst of gunshots from inside the house.

Longarm hadn't thought there was any glass left in those windows to break. But there was.

Glass flew outward.

So did the preacher.

"Shit!" the startled preacher yelped.

With one hand holding his Bible and the other securing his hat he went scampering off to the side with a mighty leap that cleared the fence and sent him atumble into the yard next door.

He did not stop running until he was somewhere out of sight.

To give the crowd its due, Longarm thought, the folks who were observing this did not laugh a whole hell of a lot.

Ben Mader gave Longarm a sorrowful look. Longarm

only shrugged. "It ain't often easy, son. An' I misdoubt they really wanted t' hurt him. Likely just scarin' him off." Longarm grinned and added, "I'd say them fellas in there is not prayerful men."

The young constable managed a smile in return. "Yes, sir, I'd have to say that you're right."

Just to remind them that the law was still outside, Longarm loosed a few shots through each window, then reloaded his Colt. Now all that needed doing, barring a breakout attempt by the kidnappers, was to get those lanterns. And wait.

"Help me get all these lanterns lighted, Ben."

Mader glanced toward the western sky, then said, "It's still a good hour, maybe hour and a half until dark, marshal."

"I'd say that that's about right, Ben." Longarm reached for a lantern, thumbed the lever to raise the globe and struck a match.

"Won't those outlaws see what you're doing?"

"Of course they will," Longarm agreed. "Firstly, by placing the lanterns now I don't have t' worry about bright light interferin' with my night vision like might could happen after dark. Second, I damn sure want those buzzards t' see. I want them t' know it's no good thinking they can wait an' slip away at night."

"You want to discourage them so they'll give up?"

Longarm nodded. "That or say to hell with it an' make their breakout attempt now. I'd be satisfied with either o' them results. Now you go on an' finish getting these lanterns lit. I'll take the tent pole you brung me an' start setting them in place. I figure I can get up against the side o' the house without much problem an' reach around in front and in back with the pole."

Ben Mader shuddered. "I'm glad it's you and not me going to be crawling around so close beside that house."

"It's all a matter o' figuring out what they can see from inside." Longarm smiled. "And what they likely can't. Now you get your pistol ready an' keep a close watch while I take care of some business here."

Chapter 20

"Is my baby in there?"

"Mrs. Palmer? What the devil are you doin' here? Get over there with the rest o' the crowd. Better yet, ma'am, you'd best go back to Miz Belton's place. I'll let you know soon as it's over."

The woman was standing, hands on hips, in the street, in plain sight from the windows of the house, more to the point in almost point-blank range should one of the men inside choose to take a shot at her.

"Ma'am. Please!"

"I do not intend to budge from this spot, Marshal. Now please answer my question. Is my daughter inside that house?"

"I'll tell you the truth, ma'am. I don't know. We haven't seen her or heard her callin' out but I can't think of anyplace else that they'd've put her."

The rest of the truth—which Longarm most assuredly did *not* want to say to Glenda Palmer's mother—was that the most likely reason kidnappers fail to use their victim as a hostage to delay pursuit would be that the victim was already dead. Otherwise, it would have been simple enough for them to put the girl on display and threaten to kill her if they were followed.

These gunmen had not done that and Longarm pretty much had to conclude that there was a strong possibility, even a probability, that Glenda had been murdered earlier, perhaps by accident or perhaps to make things more convenient for the kidnappers. After all, their messages to Congressman Howard Palmer would take place over a great distance. Glenda would not have to be put on display for that. Dammit. "Go on now, ma'am. Please."

Elspeth Palmer sniffed—it sounded more like a derisive snort but then the woman was a lady and therefore not one to snort—and tossed her head impatiently. "Do not presume to instruct me," she told the deputy.

Longarm turned to young Mader and said, "Constable, would you please escort Mrs. Palmer back to Mr. Belton's house. I'm sure they are worried about her."

"Yes, sir, but I . . ." Mader stopped and motioned with his chin to a point somewhere behind Longarm. "Where's she going, sir?"

"Huh? Who . . . ?" Longarm glanced over his shoulder and was aghast to see Elspeth Palmer marching defiantly past the water trough, through the gate which the preacher had left open earlier and up onto the porch.

She was already on the porch steps before Longarm recovered from the surprise and headed after her.

Elspeth crossed the porch and raised her hand to knock on the door.

Longarm came flying after her.

He covered the distance from the gate to the porch in three strides and launched himself forward, one arm hooking around Elspeth Palmer's waist and his revolver in the other hand.

Elspeth shrieked as Longarm swept her to the side and took her down with him onto the porch floor.

Three shots rang out from inside the house and splinters were blown out of the front door.

"Dear God. If I had been standing there . . ."

"I asked you t' go, dammit. Now d' you see why?"

"Well . . . yes."

Longarm was lying stretched full length on the porch, Elspeth Palmer partially under him.

Oddly, the militant suffragette felt downright soft and girly despite her stern and haughty appearance. Longarm could not help but notice that. Could not avoid either the hard-on that began prodding the lady's thigh. His only hope was that under these rather strained circumstances she did not notice it. Certainly she did not say anything about it. But then neither did she shift away from it.

She hadn't noticed, Longarm concluded. Good.

"Lemme get you out o' here," Longarm said. "Can you crawl on your hands an' knees? Just follow me, ma'am."

Elspeth reached up and fumbled with her hat. The feathered creation was disarranged but at least it had stayed on her head. Pinned into her hair, Longarm could see from this close up, his nose being practically inside her left ear.

"Follow me, ma'am, an' I'll . . ."

Longarm rolled onto his back and tilted up the muzzle of his Colt as a man showed himself in the window beneath which Longarm and Mrs. Palmer lay.

The outlaw was young and clean-shaven and he had a large-caliber revolver in his hand. He was looking down at the two invaders lying there on the porch. That was all Longarm had time to see. He tipped the muzzle of his Colt upward and triggered a shot intended for the fellow's chest.

Longarm's slug flew high, entering the underside of the man's chin and blowing on through the top of his skull. The bullet took an awful lot of brain and blood with it.

The dead man dropped out of sight.

Longarm gave Elspeth a shove to keep her flat on the floor while he rose to a kneeling position.

A second gunman leaped to the same window. Longarm fired and so did Ben Mader from out on the street. Puffs of dust flew from the front of the man's shirt as two bullets tore into his chest, both placed over the place where his heart should be.

That fellow spun away from the window and fell out of sight.

"Shit!" Longarm complained. He came to his feet and peered inside the house. The only people he could see in there were the two dead men on the floor close to the window. He could neither see nor hear any other threats.

"Ben."

"Yes, sir?"

"Watch out for the lady." Without waiting for a response from the constable, Longarm stepped through the open window—all vestiges of the glass that once was there had long since been blown away.

Colt held ready, he nudged each of the bodies in the ass to make sure they were really dead. A man can play possum to fake being dead but he cannot control his body's automatic reflexes, and a poke in the asshole will instantly and always result in a tightening of the buttock muscles. These fellows' butts remained relaxed and relatively soft. There was no doubt they were goners, both of them.

Satisfied there would be no one springing up behind him, Longarm very carefully went through the house.

There were only four rooms, two at the front and another two, the kitchen and a tiny bedroom, in the back.

Longarm fully expected to at least find Glenda—or her body—in the bedroom. There was no one there. No one anywhere else in the tiny house. Not Glenda. Not a third kidnapper. No one.

He even looked under the furniture and inside the icebox and the kitchen range.

Nothing.

Muttering, and more than a little surprised, Longarm, very, very carefully, not wanting to be shot by mistake, motioned at the back door for Jason Gilmore, then returned to the front of the house to let Ben know that everything was secure.

He found Mader kneeling in the bushes beside the body of fellow constable Sam Whistler.

Whistler was dead from one slug taken low in the gut. He looked like he had been a clean-cut young fellow, much like Ben Mader. Likely the two had been friends. Ben seemed to have that situation well enough in hand. Longarm turned to look for Elspeth Palmer.

He was not looking forward to delivering the news that there was no sign of Glenda anywhere inside that house.

Chapter 21

Longarm watched as Mr. and Mrs. Belton tenderly led a distraught Elspeth Palmer away. Jason assigned Ben Mader to accompany and to guard the lady. Longarm suspected Jason wanted to give Ben something to do as much as he wanted protection for the Beltons.

"He never shot anybody before," Jason said. "I don't think he ever so much as saw anybody get killed before today."

"You don't have t' worry about the boy," Longarm told him. "He had a case o' the jitters t' start with but he got over that right quick. Did everything I asked him to an' when that one there in the blue shirt stepped up ready to shoot, Ben's bullet hit right beside mine. He shot quick and true when the time came for it. He's gonna make a fine officer."

"I'll tell the chief you said that."

"Do. He needs t' hear it." Longarm smiled and reached for a cheroot. "You can tell him I said the same about you if you don't think he'd suspicion that you was lyin'."

"If you mean that, Longarm, I would take it as a high compliment."

"I mean it." Longarm scratched a match aflame and

107

touched it to the tip of his cigar. Lord, that smoke tasted good. He looked down at the pair of bodies on the floor. They were not pretty. Sudden death can distort a man's features and seems to shrink the remains. They looked like blood-soaked, oversized rag dolls sprawled there on the bare floor of the wood-frame house. "I don't recognize either o' these two," he said. "D'you?"

"Not by name but I've seen them around town, drinking and whoring and making nuisances of themselves. They seemed to have plenty of money and were willing to spend it."

Longarm knelt and went through the men's pockets. "Plenty of money, indeed," he said, pulling a wad of brand new currency from the shirt pocket of the one closer to the window and an almost identical fold of paper money from a pants pocket of the other one. "Fifties," he said with a frown. "You don't see all that many fifty dollar bills floating around. These boys seem to 've cornered the market on 'em. There must be three, four thousand dollars in each wad here an' all of it in fifties an' all of them brand spanking new."

"Odd," Jason said.

"I'll tell you something that's odder," Longarm said. "These boys show up in Cheyenne about three weeks ago, did they?"

"Yes, but how could you know that?"

"Three weeks ago five robbers hit a bank money shipment on a train in Nevada. Three of them was shot dead but two got away with more 'n twenty thousand dollars in brand new, never-been-issued fifties. We got a flyer on it back at the office. The marshal warned all of us t' be on the lookout for the money an' the robbers. I think we done stumbled into them here."

Gilmore delicately explored inside his nose with a fingertip for a few moments, as if that would assist with his thought process, then said, "Train robbers and kidnappers, too? Busy boys, ain't they?"

"I doubt the average train robber much gives a shit about political stuff. Or who holds the rights to what land."

"Then they must have been hired by someone else."

"Obviously," Longarm said, "an' that someone has Glenda now. These boys may've kidnapped her from the Belton house, but if they did they turned her over to somebody else right quick. You know what, Jason? I got an idea. Would you mind takin' over here while I traipse off an' follow a hunch?"

"I can handle it."

"Good. Thanks." Longarm took one more long look at the two dead men, then headed back outside, stretching his legs once he reached the street.

Chapter 22

"I heard shooting. What was that about?" the old man asked, pushing weakly at the porch floor to get his rocking chair started in motion.

Longarm pulled a matching rocker close and helped himself to a seat. "Ran into what looked t' be some train robbers."

"Recent?"

"About three weeks."

"The currency shipment holdup?" old Tom Harmon asked.

"That's the one. Obviously you've heard about it."

Harmon nodded. "Of course. I have friends. I keep up with things. My legs are about gone, sonny, but there's nothing wrong with my mind." He grinned. "Yet."

"That's why I wanted t' talk with you, Tom. You might could help me out."

The old man reached under his lap robe and pulled one of his cap and ball Navy Colts out into the open.

"Not that kind o' help," Longarm quickly added. Harmon looked disappointed but his revolver disappeared beneath the robe. "I noticed that your place is on a straight line between the Belton house and the place where these jaspers was holed up, and nobody with a grain of sense is gonna parade a kidnap victim through the streets any more 'n he has to."

"Meaning they should have come past me," Harmon finished the thought for him.

"Yes, sir. Meaning exactly that."

"I already told you I didn't see the girl." Harmon winked. "Believe me, I would've noticed a pretty girl walking by. I'm too old to do much but I am not so old as to not think about it. No, I did not see that girl. I'm sure of it."

"It's not the girl I have in mind, sir. Like you said, she could've been hid. But the kidnappers, at least one of 'em, would've had t' be in plain sight if they passed this way."

"You are right about that, I think. What did these boys look like?"

Longarm described the dead men in considerable detail including the clothes they were wearing and their weapons. When he was done the old man shook his head. "No one like that came past here today."

"You're sure of that, sir?"

"Positive. I would have seen them and I would remember. They did not come this way."

"An' that puzzles me, Tom."

"Know what it looks like to me, son?"

Longarm smiled. "Prob'ly the same thing it looks like t' me but we won't know that for certain sure until you tell me what you suspicion."

"It appears to me, Deputy, that you and our Cheyenne constables stumbled over that pair of train robbers almost by accident. You were searching for some criminals and indeed you found some. Except the ones you found were not the same ones that you were looking for. It looks to me as if you wound up wasting the entire afternoon, at least as far as your kidnapping is concerned. You just gave the kidnappers that many more hours to effect their getaway. They could be miles out of town by now or hiding somewhere in the city."

Longarm grunted. "Yes, sir. That's the way I'm seein' it, too."

"Do you want a suggestion?" the old man said.

"Of course."

"Alert the railroad to have all their telegraph agents within, say, fifty miles be on the lookout for any messages addressed to the girl's daddy or to her mother. I know the railroad will be cooperative. After all, you did them a large favor this afternoon when you killed those two train robbers and recovered at least some of the loot from that Nevada holdup. They are in your debt. You should also alert the post office to watch for any mail addressed to either the father or the mother. That will be more difficult, of course. There are an awful lot of substations and authorized agents. Almost every little general store out here will accept mail. But it is worth a try."

"I hadn't thought about putting the word out t' the postal stations, there bein' so many of 'em. But you're right. It can't hurt, can it?"

"A slim chance is better than none. Try it."

"I will. Thank you. It's coming night. D'you want me to . . . I dunno . . . help you inside or anything like that?"

"Thank you, but I will stay here where I can see and hear and where friends can find me. I sleep in my chair here most nights when the weather is fine. I make do quite nicely." Harmon smiled. "But I do thank you for the thoughtfulness of your offer."

"I may come back an' pick your brain again," Longarm

said. "Seems like talkin' to you about things makes me put my thoughts in order. You know what I mean?"

"Yes, of course. And do come back, Longarm, anytime at all."

When they shook good-bye, Harmon's hand felt like little more than skin, bone and sinew but it was still firm and steady as was his gaze. He met Longarm's eyes straight on.

Longarm liked the old goat and that was a fact.

He left the porch and made his way through the gate and out onto the street. Night was falling now and he was no closer to finding Glenda Palmer's kidnappers than he had been the first moment he heard about her disappearance.

Chapter 23

Longarm was tired. Hell, he was worn out. It was not physical fatigue that had him down. He hadn't had all that strenuous a day. No, the thing that had him worn down was his own view of himself.

In plain language, he had fucked up.

Glenda Palmer was kidnapped and where was her protector at the time it was happening? Why, he was sitting in the Hungry Dog saloon slopping down rye whiskey and playing cards, that's where.

Deputy United States Marshal Custis Long was, in short, responsible for Glenda's disappearance.

And it was not helping a damn thing that the post office was closed for the night so he could not get the message out about postmasters watching out for possible ransom notes.

The railroad, just like old Tom Harmon predicted, was eager to cooperate. They sent messages up and down the line by telegraph, alerting station agents, conductors and train crews alike to the kidnapping and asking them to report suspicious people, ransom messages or anything else they might stumble across.

There was no way to know how much good that would do—if any—but he had to at least try to do something right in this case.

Lordy! Sitting right there in the damn Hungry Dog drinking whiskey and playing poker.

What was Billy Vail going to say when he found out? Longarm figured his best course of action would be to first get Glenda the hell back with her mother where she belonged; second, he needed to get this thing completely wrapped up before Billy got so much as a whiff of the stink Longarm had made with the case.

He shook his head and jammed the smoldering butt of a cheroot into his jaw while he reached for the tin of solvent and greasy rag he always carried in his gear. He dipped a wire brush in the solvent and ran it several times through the barrel of his Colt, then through each chamber of the cylinder that also lay on the table before him. He followed the brush with dry cloth patches speared on the end of the stubby cleaning rod and then with some oiled patches. By the time he was done cleaning the .45 inside and out it gleamed with a fresh application of light, sweet oil. Longarm preferred to use sewing machine oil on his weapons rather than the heavier, stickier stuff sold as gun oil. Regular gun oil was better for storage purposes. But Longarm cleaned his firearms often and with meticulous care, and he wanted nothing gummy or heavy with trapped dust that might in any way slow the speed of the mechanical action. After all, his life could well depend on it.

When he was done cleaning the .45 he dropped it back into the holster that was hanging on the headboard of the room in the banker's big home. He blew out the lamp and walked to the window where he stood peering out into the darkness while he finished his smoke.

Glenda was out there. Somewhere. Possibly dead. Almost certainly in a state of terror if she were still alive.

And it was his damned fault. His. His alone. If only he had been tending to business the way he ought to. . . .

He was still standing there when he heard the faint click of a latch and saw a patch of yellow light emerge and grow as the door into the hallway swung silently open.

Longarm's immediate reaction was to lift the Colt from its holster.

Then he saw who his visitor was and the revolver dropped back into the leather.

The figure was shrouded and ghostly but this was no specter come a-calling in the night. This was the same flesh and blood female who had visited him the previous night.

She must have been waiting for the glow of lamplight to disappear at the foot of his door before she entered. He doubted she expected to find him still awake and beside the window rather than lying in bed.

She meant him no harm. That was immediately plain as she lifted the hem of her robe and started to kneel on the side of the bed, obviously expecting to find him there.

When she did not she turned, wheeling to face him there at the window. Longarm guessed she found it difficult to see due to the layer of thin, almost transparent gauze veil draped over her chapeau, otherwise she surely would have spotted him to begin with.

"Good evening," he said, reaching down to flick the stub of his cigar out the window.

He smiled. "That answers one question anyhow. Now I know it wasn't Glenda who slipped in here last night. That don't leave too many others for me t' pick from in guessing who you be."

"You really did not know?"

"No, but now I do."

"My voice," she said. "It is recognizable?"

"I oughta be able t' tell it. I been hearing it enough lately with all them speeches you been giving."

"I am not a handsome woman," Elspeth Palmer said, admitting the obvious. "Nor am I young." Older than Longarm probably, he guessed.

"But I have needs."

"Yes, I reckon you do."

"My husband . . ." She sighed. "We have been married a very long time. Our interests have diverged. He has needs, too, but society, inequitable as always, finds that only natural. The world excuses his mistresses and his casual liaisons. It would condemn me for mine. Do I disgust you?"

"No," Longarm said. The woman did not particularly excite him. But then that was not what she asked. "Your marriage is your business, ma'am."

"You are virile, and when I saw you shoot that man . . ." Despite the way she was bundled up he could see her shudder. "I felt something stir in my loins when you did that. The raw power of it. The . . . I don't know what else. But something. Something was there. I felt it. If I were young I would want to have your baby. If I had any milk for you to drink I would want you to suckle at my breast. I knew I had to taste you. I want to feel you inside my body again. Will you do that for me, Deputy Long? Will you take me to bed and expend some of that power upon me?" She took a long, deep breath. "Please?"

She was not a good-looking woman but it would take one cold, mean son of a bitch to say no to a proposition as plain as that.

Longarm started unbuttoning his shirt.

Chapter 24

Elspeth's body had the heavy fullness of maturity with melon breasts, a thick waist with a roll of fat around it and thighs like large hams. Beautiful she was not. But she made every effort to make up for that with the passion she brought to the coupling.

"Let me. Shh, shh . . . no, let me. Please."

Longarm lay back. And let her.

She struck a match and lighted the bedside lamp, then sat on the side of the bed and enjoying the view, her eyes caressing his lean, muscular frame. "Oh, my. You're so . . . so . . . oh, my."

Lightly, hesitantly, she touched his cock. It was not exactly flaccid but he was far from being fully aroused yet. Elspeth ran her fingertips over it very gently, then bent and took him into her mouth.

Longarm reckoned that someday, perhaps when he was old and gray, he might find himself in some woman's mouth and he would fail to grow hard there.

But if that was ever going to happen it was a helluva long way off from now, he figured.

His manhood filled and grew hard in her mouth. When she lifted her head, the blood rushed through his penis and glistened wetly in the lamplight from her saliva.

"It is beautiful, isn't it," Elspeth exclaimed. She touched it lightly on the dark, bulbous head, delighted at the way his prick bounced in response. She laughed happily at the sight of it bobbing ever so slightly up and down in time with the heartbeats that filled it.

"It really is beautiful," she whispered, then bent low and again took him into her mouth.

Longarm reached down to her tits, fondling and squeezing and rubbing them.

He took a nipple between thumb and forefinger, rolling and twisting. Elspeth began to squirm and wriggle and her breathing became difficult. She shuddered and acted like she was having some sort of spasm. He was still inside her mouth and for a moment was afraid she might be having some sort of fit. It wouldn't much do to have her bite while he was in there.

"Are you all right?"

She stopped quivering and lifted her face off his cock. "I just . . . I just . . . dear God, I just had one of those . . . what do you call them? Orgasm? I just had one of those."

Elspeth began to cry, her shoulders shaking with emotion. Longarm pulled her down onto the bed beside him, stroking her shoulders and the back of her head.

"I just . . ."

"It's all right, Elspeth. Really." He stroked her some more, gentling her like he would a young and skittish colt, and slowly the sobbing began to subside.

"Are you all right now?" he asked when he felt reasonably sure she was done with whatever this had been.

"I heard . . . all my life I heard whispers. The servants,

you know. They like to talk. And girls at school, the bold ones, they talked about the . . . those climax things. They talked about what it felt like but I . . . I never felt anything like that.

"I bore Howard a child and had two others stillborn. I have tried to be a good wife to him. But he . . . I never felt anything like this." She buried her face beneath the shelf of his jaw, her breath warm on his neck. "Never," she whispered.

Longarm patted her back and shoulders and with one hand cupped the back of her head and stroked the hair there.

Her sobbing aroused him and he gently turned her over so that she lay on the bed with his lean body on top of her. He reached down to her crotch. She was dripping wet there. He fingered the opening and Elspeth cried out and clutched him tight with her arms.

"Open," he said. "Open up for me."

The blind snake had been thoroughly aroused and while Elspeth Palmer might well have reached her satisfaction, Custis Long damn sure had not. Yet. "Open your legs," he mumbled.

She did and he levered himself over her. Then down. Probing. Seeking. Finding the moist portal to a world of pleasure and sliding inside. Gentle for that first penetration. Even so Elspeth gasped when her body was asked to accommodate an object that large.

She cried out, the sound muffled against his shoulder, and she held him in a fierce embrace.

After a moment he could feel the tension go out of her and he began to stroke slowly in and out.

Then faster. Harder. Faster still. Bucking and plunging.

Elspeth hung on for dear life, clinging to him with arms and legs.

He could feel her body again responding, could feel it in the way her pussy clenched and trembled, could feel it in the heat and quickness of her breath, could hear it in the low, keening moan that rose and fell somewhere deep in her throat.

Elspeth exploded, going rigid beneath him, almost at the same moment that Longarm reached his own deep, shuddering climax.

Hot juices spurted out of him, filling her cavity and flowing out around the powerful obstruction that blocked that opening to her body.

His jism seeped out and dripped onto his balls, tickling when it slid off onto the sheet.

"Oh, dear. Oh, God," Elspeth muttered over and over again. "Never. In my life. Now . . . twice. In one night. Oh, dear."

He gave her time to recover, then rolled off of her and reached onto the nightstand for a cheroot.

The flare of the match gave him a look at her: a sagging middle-aged woman with skin mottled and blotchy in the aftermath of her passions, a woman who was none too handsome to begin with. But by damn a satisfied woman.

And the truth was that he was well satisfied himself. His balls were lighter now. Even if his crotch and his bed were wet. Dammit.

He got up and began looking for one of those little hand towels that the Beltons laid out for their guests. He needed to do some cleaning up before he could get to sleep and he figured Elspeth did, too.

"Are you all right?" he asked.

"Yes." She sat up and swung her legs off the bed. "I'm fine. I . . . thank you, Deputy."

Longarm grinned. "I think maybe you could call me by my name now."

"I . . . dear God. I've forgotten what your first name is. I mean . . . of all things. And I don't know your *name*?"

Longarm laughed. And reminded her. Hell, he understood. His name just hadn't been important to her before.

Now he reckoned it was. "Go back t' bed," he said gently. "Get yourself some sleep."

"But . . . Glenda. What about Glenda?"

"We'll find her." He said the words firmly and with conviction. The truth of course was that he had no idea if they would ever find the girl and less hope that they would get her back alive.

He did not want to tell her mother that.

"We'll get her back," he declared.

"Thank you." She smiled a little, then reached out to turn down the wick on his lamp until it sputtered out and the room was again in darkness. "Thank you."

He could hear the rustle of cloth as she found her nightdress and managed to get into it.

Then she was gone, the shift of the bed telling him when she got up and a pale glow of light from the hall filling the room as she slipped out and hurried barefoot back to her own room in the banker's big house.

Chapter 25

Breakfast, it seemed, was a family affair and Custis Long was invited. He did not have time for a proper barbershop shave and did not feel inclined to shave himself with no mirror available—a man could cut his own throat that way if he wasn't careful—so he dressed and went downstairs, stubble and all. As it was he was the last one to appear in the dining room. He slid into the one chair that had a place setting of tableware, it being across the table from Elspeth.

This was the first good opportunity Longarm had to get acquainted with the master of this manor. Will Belton was a tall, distinguished man with steel gray hair, a portly build, jowls to match and untrimmed snow white eyebrows.

"It's kind o' you to invite me t' your table," Longarm said, unfolding his napkin and tucking it into his shirt collar.

"You are our guest, and it is our pleasure to have you," Belton lied. He was smooth about it though. Longarm had to give him that. But if it weren't for the threats against the Palmers there was no way an ordinary lawman like Custis Long would ever sit at the banker's breakfast table being served steak, ham and fried chicken by a maidservant.

Damned fine-looking steak and ham, too, although if

125

pressed he might have been forced to admit that the chicken could have benefited from being rolled around in flour before it was fried. He liked it best that way.

He reached for a bowl of fried potatoes, then stopped short of grabbing it when he realized that no one else was eating. They were all sitting there looking at him.

Longarm cleared his throat and loosened his shoulders and pulled his hand back away from the spuds.

"When you are ready," Belton said.

"Sorry."

Everyone bowed their heads and folded their hands— even the serving girl Maria; Longarm peeked—and Will Belton launched into a long-winded prayer that had more to do with the state of Wyoming Territory's economy than it did with the grub they were fixing to eat. But then that sort of shit probably meant the world to Belton and his sort while Custis Long and ordinary folk like him were satisfied if they could just keep their bellies filled.

"Is there anything you would care to add, Mr. Long?" Belton offered when his prayer was concluded.

"No, sir. Well, other than we get Glenda home safe an' sound."

"Oh. I should have mentioned that, shouldn't I?" the banker said.

Longarm certainly thought he should have but he did not criticize the gentleman's prayer. He kept his mouth shut and reached for those potatoes again. This time he snagged them and piled a healthy heap of them onto his plate while Will Belton was busy accepting a choice steak from Maria who hovered close by, attending to her employer's needs.

They were about done with breakfast, the plates cleared

away and coffee being poured from an ornate silver pitcher, when there was a pounding at the front door.

The knocking continued until Maria set the coffeepot down without finishing filling all their cups and hurried to answer the door. Moments later a boy, ten or eleven years old with his face flushed red by exertion and excitement and with a little round messenger cap falling down over his ears, came shyly into the room.

He looked along the breakfast table like he'd never seen anything so grand—as indeed he probably had not—then remembered his task and came not to Will Belton but to Longarm.

"I's told t' give this t' you, sir."

"To me?"

"You's the marshal, ain't you?"

"Yes, of course."

The boy thrust an envelope into Longarm's hand, then whirled around and escaped from this unfamiliar territory. He did not even wait to collect a tip for his services.

Longarm shrugged and examined the envelope while Maria returned to filling the coffee cups as if there had been no interruption.

The letter was addressed not to him but to *Mrs. Elspeth Palmer, c/o the Belton House*. There was no street, city or territory spelled out on the envelope nor was there a return address or even a stamp.

"Since this is addressed to you, Miz Palmer, I expect I should get your permission t' open it." He wanted to be the one to read the message just in case it was the sort of thing that should be softened a mite before being presented to a mother whose child is in danger.

"You have it, of course."

"Thank you, ma'am."

Longarm reached into his pocket for his knife and sliced the envelope open. There was a single sheet of folded paper inside.

Penciled in large, block letters was the brief message: STOP THE MADNESS IN WASHINGTON OR THE GIRL WILL DIE.

At least it wasn't anything graphically threatening. He reckoned Elspeth could handle seeing this. After all, it was what they were all expecting anyway. Frowning, he handed the message to her.

"I must inform Howard about this," she said. Elspeth Palmer was a tough woman. Rather than being devastated by the threat it seemed to have tapped into wells of firm resolve somewhere within her.

"I'll walk with you to the depot," Longarm said.

"Thank you." She looked down at the paper in her hand. "Glenda did not write this note, you know."

"Are you sure?"

"Positive. The handwriting on the envelope is hers. I would recognize it anywhere. But someone else wrote the note itself. Is that significant?"

"Maybe," Longarm said. "No way t' know at this point."

"Is there anything we can do?" Idamae Belton asked.

"Nothing that I can think of," Longarm answered the wife but his attention was on the banker who seemed almost disinterested, as if he did not very much care what happened to his wife's associates. Not a supporter of the suffrage movement? Longarm wondered. Possibly. Or the man might simply have gas pains from all that beef he put away at breakfast and not want to show it.

"If there is anything . . . let us know. Please."

"Yes, ma'am."

"Isn't that right, William? William!"

"What? Oh, yes. Quite right, dear. Quite right."

Longarm doubted that Belton had the least idea what it was he was agreeing with there.

He pushed his chair back from the table, leaving untouched that freshly poured coffee with its rich wonderful aroma. Dammit.

"If you're ready, ma'am, we'll go send that telegram t' your husband, then I have some things I'd like t' do."

"In conjunction with . . . this?" She waved the note.

"Yes, ma'am."

Elspeth picked up her handbag and stuffed the envelope into it, then squared her shoulders and said, "I am ready, Marshal Long."

Chapter 26

Longarm paused at the Union Pacific district superinten-
dent's door. Mrs. Palmer was at the counter overseeing the
transmission of her message to her husband after first letting Longarm read and approve it.

"Excuse me," he said to the Union Pacific boss. "I want
you t' instruct all your telegraphers. Any messages relating
to the kidnapping, even messages that you suspect might
be, like in code or whatever, anything coming in or going
out it don't matter, you have a copy brought to me right
off, will you? Send a message runner and don't dawdle
about it."

"Is that an instruction, Deputy?"

"Sir, you know good an' well you work for the railroad,
not for the government. I ain't got the authority t' give you
orders. Congressman Palmer might have some sort of authority dependin' on what committees he sits on, but I
wouldn't know about that. All I am is a simple deputy
United States marshal." He paused and gave the man a cold
look. "And I'm just askin'. Not making a report to the congressman, just askin' as polite as I know how. Now do we
understand each other?"

"Of course I intend to cooperate fully, Deputy."

"Thank you, sir. I'll be sure an' let Congressman Palmer know how helpful you an' the Union Pacific have been about his only daughter bein' kidnapped. Thank you very much." He touched the brim of his hat in a pretense of politeness—pompous asshole—and turned to see if Mrs. Palmer was done with her chore.

"All set?" he asked.

"Yes. They said they will rush delivery of the message. Howard will know within an hour or so." She sighed.

"Feeling all right?"

"I am a little shaky but I shall be all right, thank you. Can we go back to Idamae's house now, please?"

"Yes, ma'am, but I'd like t' swing by the police station first. It's only a block or two out o' the way."

"As you wish." Elspeth Palmer picked up her umbrella and gathered her skirts. Her chin was up and she seemed determined to maintain her composure, no matter what. Longarm admired that. There was more to Elspeth than met the eye. She was one tough old broad. And you wouldn't think it to look at her but she could fuck like a rabbit once her corset came off and her hair came down.

He offered the lady his arm and escorted her out into the bright sunshine of a cloudless Wyoming morning.

"Dammit, Jason, d'you mean to tell me that your police chief *still* ain't come back?"

"I'm afraid not, Longarm. We received a wire this morning saying he is going on to San Francisco."

"Did he say when he'll be back?"

"No. He said I am to remain in charge until his return."

"Does he know that a congressman's daughter has been kidnapped here?"

The constable sighed. "To tell you the truth, I suspect that is the reason he hasn't returned. He can't be held responsible for anything that happens when he is away. If you see what I mean."

"Yeah, I do, dammit."

"So is there any way I can help you in his place?" Jason Gilmore asked.

"There sure is. I need t' be free to look for these sons o' bitches, but my hands are tied as long as I got t' be sticking close to Mrs. Palmer. I was hoping you could assign me one o' your officers to handle that for the next little while. An' if it makes a difference, I can deputize him t' help me and give him a voucher for a dollar and a half a day for as long as it takes t' clear this mess."

Jason rubbed the side of his nose in thought for a moment, then grunted. "I know just the man for you. His wife is expecting and they can use the extra money."

The Cheyenne copper turned out to be a round-faced fellow in his thirties named Donald Wexler. Jason performed the introductions.

"I'm ready to do anything you need, Marshal," Wexler said. "Just tell me what you need."

"Jason says you're a reliable man an' I'll take his word for that," Longarm said. "I want you t' draw a shotgun an' a pouch of double-ought shells for it, and I want you t' keep something firm in mind. Anybody comes at Mrs. Palmer, you put him on the ground. Don't try an' sweep his legs out from under him. Shoot for the belly. Shoot to kill the bastard."

Wexler's eyes went wide. "Are you serious?"

"Dead serious," Longarm assured him. "As dead as I'd expect him t' be when you get done with him."

The police officer looked a trifle queasy at the thought but he took a deep breath then nodded. "I understand, sir."

Longarm beckoned for Elspeth to join them in the privacy of the chief's office. He explained the situation and turned her over to Donald Wexler with the assurance that he would see her later in the day.

"That's better," Longarm said once Elspeth and a heavily armed Constable Wexler were on their way to the Belton house. "Now I can move around however I need."

"Is there anything I can do to help?" Jason asked.

"I don't think of anything right at this moment, but if I do I'll call on you for it." Longarm smiled at the young officer. "You don't look like such-a-much, kid, but you are damn sure all right in my book."

Gilmore looked startled by the compliment. And very pleased.

"I'll see you later, Jason." Longarm headed outside and stretched his legs in the direction of the Cheyenne Post Office.

Chapter 27

Not many towns could boast of independent, full-time post offices, most relying on substations in stores or even saloons, but Cheyenne had its own genuine postal facility. Longarm had never asked but assumed that would be because the railroad brought mail to Cheyenne that was ultimately destined for half of Wyoming Territory and probably parts of Nebraska and northern Colorado, too.

In some ways that made his current question more difficult, which he knew when he approached the postmaster and posed it.

"Thanks for spotting this and sending it over to me, sir. It's mighty helpful and I appreciate it. My question now is, d'you have any idea who mailed it or when or where? Any small scrap of information might be helpful here."

"I wish I could tell you more, Marshal. We have half a dozen mail boxes sited around the city," the gentleman said. "This letter was dropped into one of them."

"D'you know which one?"

The postmaster, a balding, bespectacled man with

bushy side whiskers, shook his head. "No, I don't. It could have been any of them."

"How 'bout when it was mailed," Longarm asked.

"I can do at least a little better with that. Mail in those boxes is collected each afternoon about five-thirty or six depending on the exact location as my carrier makes his rounds. The evening mail is sorted overnight so it is ready to go out the next morning, either on city delivery routes or on a train. The morning eastbound runs at four-thirty-seven and the westbound about two hours later.

"There are other daytime collections about seven-thirty, ten-thirty, twelve-thirty and two o'clock. Those are sorted and sent out by the next available means, whether rail or coach. This envelope came in with the seven-thirty pickup. The carrier didn't notice it, but a clerk on the sorting table spotted it. He saw that it had no stamp. That's what made him look closer. Fortunately, he remembered the notice I posted yesterday about mail addressed to either of the Palmers."

"You put up a note about that?"

"After you asked us to be on the lookout for the ad-dressee, yes. And it paid off. My clerk brought the enve-lope to me and I immediately had the boy take it to you."

"Which I damn sure appreciate," Longarm said.

"At any rate, the best I can do is to tell you that this note was dropped into one of our boxes sometime be-tween five-thirty yesterday afternoon and seven-thirty this morning."

"Did you ask the carrier if he noticed this envelope when he collected the mail this morning?"

"I asked. He says he did not."

Longarm sighed. "It was worth askin'."

"If it helps," the postmaster offered, "I can tell you that the note was posted within the city. Mail brought in from elsewhere is sorted at a different table."

"An' that could be plenty helpful," Longarm said.

Glenda's handwriting could have been placed on that envelope at any time, of course, and the note added later. But the odds now were good that the girl and her kidnappers were still somewhere in or very near Cheyenne.

And that suggested that she was very likely still alive, it being damned difficult to dispose of a body in an area that was close to houses. Small boys, for instance, are notoriously curious. Cats have nothing on a ten-year-old kid when it comes to snooping into anything new or strange or different.

On the other hand, kidnappers who hoped to hide their victim in an urban area always have to worry about noise. A scream will draw attention quite as readily as a pool of blood. And the dead are not going to make any unwanted noises.

Longarm thanked the postmaster and headed for the front door of the post office. In the lobby, however, he slowed and drifted to a halt.

Longarm rubbed the back of his neck and pondered the little that he had learned. What he knew and what he could reasonably surmise. Glenda could well be held prisoner somewhere on the outskirts of Cheyenne. It was possible. Not a certainty but still a chance.

He wondered if he should bother Jason and his few available police officers with this slim likelihood. They could conduct another search. But . . . for exactly what? They could not burst into homes or even businesses without warrants. Dammit!

Longarm pulled the note from his pocket and stared at it again. If only the thing could talk.

The writing was in pencil, not ink. The paper, however, was of decent quality. Not bond—he held it up to the light from a nearby window and looked; there was no watermark—but it was not cheap foolscap either.

There was something about the lettering that bothered him though. Something about it seemed not quite right.

The note was written in careful block letters. The paper was unlined but the wording was perfectly level, suggesting that some sort of straightedge had been used as an aid to the writing. A ruler or another piece of paper perhaps. And the pencil strokes were perfectly vertical, giving no indication of whether the writer was right- or left-handed.

"Stop the madness in Washington or the girl will die," Longarm muttered aloud.

Stop the madness. No specification of which madness. That knowledge was assumed. Fair enough, Longarm conceded. The reference was indeed understood. But . . . madness? Somehow the word choice did not seem appropriate here. Certainly this was unlike any ransom note or threat he had ever seen before.

There was no . . . there was no *bluster* involved.

Whoever wrote this note was self-assured. The straight, unwavering pencil lines, none of them especially heavy or hurried, suggested someone who was in control.

The threat itself was not emphasized. The writer took it for granted that he would be believed.

"Shit!" Longarm snarled aloud. The remark drew a glance of sharp rebuke from an old biddy who was fumbling in her handbag for the key to her delivery box.

"Shit," he repeated, louder this time and entirely deliberate about it. This time the holier-than-thou old cunt tossed her head and sniffed. Loudly.

Longarm jammed the note into his pocket and got the hell out of there before he vented his anger by slapping the bitch. All of a sudden he was just in that sort of mood so it was time to move along. Quickly.

Chapter 28

Feeling like pure hell, Longarm sulked and grumbled his way out past the cattle pens and in a wide sweep around the south end of town, then back to the Belton house where he found Elspeth, Idamae and Constable Wexler in the parlor. There was no sign of Maria or of the cook Martha but some mighty tantalizing smells were drifting out of the kitchen along with the clatter of pans and utensils. Longarm hadn't realized how time had slipped away while he walked. And thought.

"Have you heard anything more?" Elspeth immediately asked. For just a fleeting moment she looked hopeful but her expression drooped when Longarm shook his head and answered, "I was hoping you had."

The four of them sat in the parlor for a spell, no one speaking. The women sat with their hands folded in their laps, knees tight together, backs straight and chins high. Just exactly the way both ladies were probably taught in finishing school. They seemed comfortable enough to sit there like china dolls. Longarm was not. He tried to read a magazine but it was some of the suffragette bullshit and he

141

really had no interest in it. The letters swam before his eyes but he did not bother to make any sense of them.

Wexler sat in an overstuffed armchair and fidgeted back and forth. The constable shifted from cheek to cheek, examined his fingernails as if they were new to him, and looked like he would rather be almost anywhere other than here.

Not that Longarm blamed him. He would rather be somewhere else, too.

It was a relief when Maria announced they could all come in to dine.

Lunch was cold chicken with some sort of fancy dressing, like the perfectly ordinary chicken meat was a fancy salad, and a jellied tomato concoction that Longarm did not recognize but which he thought tasted like shit and was probably spoiled. He noticed Wexler did not eat any of his either but both ladies professed to enjoy it. Tomato aspic Idamae Belton called it.

Longarm hurried through the meal, then rose. "If you'll excuse me, ladies, I'd like t' step out onto the porch for a few minutes. Wanna come along, Don?"

"If you think it would be all right, sir."

"We'll be right outside those windows," Longarm told the women. "Holler if you need us. An' that isn't just an expression. I mean it. If you see or hear or even just imagine anything out o' the ordinary, raise your voices loud as you can an' call out. We'll come runnin'."

"Oh, what could happen to us here?" Idamae said. "We're safe as clams in the house."

"Ma'am, I seem t' recall that Glenda was in this house when she was grabbed so if you don't mind I'll say it again. Anything goes wrong, you sing out. Don an' me will come."

"Oh!" Idamae turned her head away and flushed beet red with embarrassment.

"Are you comin', officer?" Longarm asked.

"Right behind you, sir."

They went out onto the front porch where Wexler refused Longarm's offer of a cheroot.

Longarm picked a rocking chair that was to his liking and settled into it, absently swaying to and fro while he trimmed and lighted a smoke for himself.

"How'd they get that girl spirited away like they done," Longarm mused at one point, "an' nobody see them do it?"

"In a railroad town like this, sir, we go full speed day and night. And it was broad daylight when the young lady was taken. My guess is that someone surely will have seen them. Our problem is that we don't know who to ask. And for their part, those witnesses don't know that they have information that could be of value."

Longarm puffed on his cheroot and rocked in silence for a moment. Then he said, "You're right, Don. Dead on target."

"Perhaps. For all the good it will do."

Longarm craned his neck from side to side, loosening tight muscles. He closed his eyes and almost appeared to sleep. After a moment his eyes snapped open and he sat bolt upright, the rocking motion halting.

"What?" Wexler said.

"Don, you're a genius."

"I am?"

"Yes. You are." Longarm stood and hurried inside.

Now if only Elspeth had a good likeness of her daughter. A photograph, a locket painting, anything would do.

Chapter 29

"This week's edition came out yesterday, Marshal. I won't be printing another until next Thursday," the ink-stained gentleman at the newspaper office told him.

"Damn. All right then. D'you issue extras?"

"This is not a big city newspaper, marshal. We don't have the resources, that is to say the advertisers, to justify anything like that."

"How about job printing? Do you print something other than your newspaper. Flyers an' things like that."

"Of course. A small newspaper could not survive without that sort of traffic."

"D'you have an artist? Somebody that can draw a likeness taken from another drawing?"

"Yes, we have a gifted artist on staff here." The fellow smiled. "If I do say so myself."

Longarm tugged a heart-shaped gold locket from his pocket and laid it on the counter between them. "Can you draw that?"

The newspaperman looked puzzled. "You want a drawing of that necklace?"

"No, of course not. I mean the picture in it." Longarm

fiddled with the locket but couldn't find the clue to getting the aggravating little sonuvabitch open. Finally the newspaper editor took it from him, examined it for a moment and opened it. Inside the locket was a small photograph, obviously cut out of a larger image that had included others in a group. "That girl there," he said, pointing. "What I want is for you t' draw a good likeness of her an' print that on a small sheet. Like a billboard or a handout flyer. You know? Could you do that?"

"Yes, of course I can, but it would cost you."

"How much?"

"What size sheet do you need, sir?"

"Hell, I dunno. This big maybe." Longarm gestured rather vaguely with his hands to indicate a size of perhaps six or seven inches square. "It ain't the size that matters. It's more important for the picture to be as recognizable as possible. Can you do that?"

"Hmm. I have some paper stock left over from another job. I could let that go cheap. Then there is my time. . . ."

"I need it in a hurry," Longarm said.

The fellow sighed. "Everyone does, sir."

"No, I mean it." He laid his wallet on the counter and opened it to display his badge. "This is official business. The girl is missing and may be in danger. I got a team of searchers standing by ready t' go hunt for the girl but they none of them ever seen her. They need to know who it is they're looking for."

"That sounds exciting. It quite frankly sounds like there may be a story in it for me."

"If you get this right out for me, friend, there might could be an exclusive in it for you an' your paper. I'll sit down with you an' tell you everything you want to know.

But first that girl needs your help t' get her found safe. Will you help me, mister?"

"Yes. Of course. It will cost . . . oh . . . how many did you say you need?"

"Not many. A couple dozen would be enough."

The man took a scrap of ink smudged newsprint and an oddly shaped, thick, slab-sided pencil and did some calculating. "I can do it for two dollars and a quarter."

"Can you have it done this afternoon?"

"Is it that important?"

"Yes, sir, it is. The girl's life could depend on it."

"In that case . . . four o'clock. I will try to have the finished product in your hands by four. No later than five."

Longarm slammed his palm down on the counter with a loud exclamation. "Good! I'll be back at four."

This should be allowable as a legitimate expense, he was thinking as he let himself out of the newspaper office and went back out onto the street. Henry would bitch and moan about the size of the bill. But Longarm was sure—reasonably so anyway—that he would pay it.

For the first time since Glenda Palmer disappeared, Longarm was optimistic about their prospects for getting her back.

Chapter 30

Five turned into five-thirty but there was still daylight in the sky when Longarm collected the handbills with a likeness of Glenda Palmer on them. The drawing was not really very good, certainly nothing that would excite the interest of a portrait artist, but it was close enough that Longarm would have recognized her. Probably.

Anyway it was the best thing available. He tucked the stack of flyers into a large envelope and paid cash for the service.

"Don't forget this," the newspaperman reminded him, handing over Elspeth Palmer's locket with the picture of Glenda inside. Longarm snapped it open and compared it with the drawing on the handbills. The gentleman had copied the photo as closely as he was able.

"Will that do?" the man asked.

Longarm gave him a small smile. "That remains t' be seen, don't it?"

"Remember what you promised."

Longarm nodded. "If this pays off, I'll come back an' give you an exclusive on the story."

"Excellent. Human interest stories always please my readers."

"Friend, if this works you'll have a story that'll be picked up in newspapers all over the country. Prob'ly over in Europe too." Longarm turned and walked out, leaving the disbelieving newspaperman behind. But then this Cheyenne newspaper publisher had no idea who it was who was missing. Or why.

"I hope you don't mind me intrudin' on you like this," Longarm said.

"Not at all. I'm glad for the company," old Tom Harmon told him. "Take a load off and have a seat if you like. Can I offer you some supper?"

"I was just going to offer you some."

"Oh, I already ate today, thank you."

"Then how's about a smoke," Longarm said. "I have some pretty nice cheroots here."

"No, thanks."

Longarm reached around to his hip pocket and produced a pint bottle of rye whiskey that he'd picked up at a saloon on his way here from the newspaper office downtown. He pulled the cork and offered the bottle to the old man.

"Now that is something that I can be tempted with." Harmon smelled the whiskey, then took a very small sip and finally, smiling, upended the bottle and took a deep swallow of rye. He smacked his lips with pleasure and returned the bottle to Longarm who also took a drink before he pushed the cork back in and handed the bottle to the old man. "In case the night gets chilly."

Harmon nodded solemnly. "We do get cold nights hereabouts, even at this time of year."

"I kinda thought you might. Mr. Harmon . . ."

"Tom. Please call me Tom."

"Yes, sir. Tom, I got a favor to ask of you."

"If I can help, I certainly will."

"I'm looking for this here girl." Longarm reached inside his coat and produced one of the last of the handbills he'd gotten printed that afternoon. "You see everything that goes on around here so I was hoping you might've spotted her going by."

"We already went through this," Harmon said. "I told you then that I saw no one in distress. Has anything changed today?"

"Yes, sir." Longarm told him about the envelope. "I seen on that envelope that it is the girl's own handwriting. Her mama says she's sure of that. An' her hand is perfectly normal. By that I mean it has all the usual loops and whorls and fussy stuff the way young women tend to write, but what seems important to me is that it ain't scrawled. The loops are fully round and very carefully formed. There's no shakiness in the handwriting. It looks like she took her time to form the letters mighty careful."

"Do you think she is faking having been kidnapped?" Harmon asked, immediately seeing the direction Longarm's comments were going.

"Possible," Longarm conceded. "Faking it or for some reason cooperating with the kidnappers. For sure it don't look to me like she's scared or real worried with her situation."

Harmon accepted the drawing and spent some time examining it but when he was done he shook his head. "No, sorry. I have not seen her pass by on my block."

"Damn."

"The question is not a waste however."

"How's that?"

"Because now you can be reasonably sure that the girl or her kidnappers did not come in this direction. You can concentrate your search toward the other end of town."

Longarm smiled. "Then I'd best get that word out to my army."

"Your what?"

The smile turned into a laugh. "I hope you don't mind but I'll have a passel of deputies reporting to me through the evenin'. I told them they can expect to find me on your front porch. If that's all right."

"Oh, it's fine with me. An army of deputies, you say? Did Marshal Vail call out every available man for this?"

"Better. An' there ain't a man among 'em," Longarm said.

"Now you do have my curiosity aroused."

"You'll see," was all Longarm would tell him though. "You will see."

Chapter 31

"Yes, what is it, son?" Longarm sat on Tom Harmon's porch, legs crossed as he leaned back in his chair. He had a cheroot in one hand and the now nearly empty bottle of rye in the other.

"Me and Richard seen a blond lady talking to Marybeth Hankin. We don't know her. Do you wanta come take a look at her, sir? Do you think it could be her?"

"How old was the blond lady, son?"

"Oh, she's old. Maybe thirty. Could be more."

"I don't think she's the lady I'm looking for. Why don't you and Richard keep on looking. You might find her."

"All right." The kid grinned and went racing back out into the street where two other small boys were waiting, too timid to come inside the fence.

"Kids?" Harmon asked when the boy and his companions were gone.

Longarm nodded. "Exactly. I got t' thinking. Who sees more or is asked less than a bunch o' damn kids. The little buggers are everywhere. They're practically like ants underfoot but nobody pays them no mind. So I thought I'd ask them. I passed out a bunch of those drawings to show what I'm looking for an' I told them they could find me here to report what they seen."

"Why here? I mean, I certainly don't mind. But why here instead of over there at the banker's house?" Harmon reached for the rye, which Longarm passed to him.

"Boys are excitable. I knew good an' well there will be a whole lot o' false reports. They'll want to tell me everything that's going on in the whole of Cheyenne. I don't want the girl's mother getting all worked up an' hopeful every time some kid comes running up with a yarn to spin. Figure it's better to wait here so I can get the stories before I bother her with any of it."

"Let's hope your idea works. What are you paying this army of yours?"

Longarm grinned. "I told them there's a five-dollar reward if they find the woman I'm looking for."

"Five dollars! It's a congressman's daughter you are looking for, isn't it? And the mother is posting a measly five dollars for a reward?"

"The mother doesn't know jack shit about it, and the reward is that size for a reason. A kid has no idea he could ever in his life get ahold of five hundred or a thousand dollars. A reward that size wouldn't mean a thing to him. But five dollars . . . now that represents all the hard rock candy in the whole wide world, and it's a number he can get his mind around. Five dollars will motivate a boy. Five hundred would be pure pie in the sky."

"Makes sense," Harmon conceded.

"If anything comes of this, and there ain't no guarantee that it will, but if anything good does come out of it I expect I can convince the mother t' set up all the kids in Cheyenne to a big ol' ice cream social."

"Now that would be a nice thing for her to do," Harmon

said. "For you to have her do." He nodded toward the street. "Maybe this is the youngster you've been looking for."

That one was not but the reports—and the boys—continued to dash in an out as the evening waned and dusk turned to darkness.

Longarm hadn't thought there could be so many kids in one town. Of course some of them kept coming back. And back again. They wanted to tell him pretty much everything they saw. Some of the things the boys saw—and reported in eager detail—would have embarrassed the hell out of their parents and their neighbors if only they had known how closely they were being observed.

Sometime after dark when most of Longarm's army of impromptu deputies were being called in for bedtime, a boy of nine or ten with the telltale shaved head that said he was just getting over an infestation of lice came through the gate and approached the men on the porch.

"Mr. Marshal, sir?"

"That would be me, son."

"That lady you're looking for?"

"Yes?"

"I know where she is, sir. She's staying at Miz Harriet Adams's rooming house. Her and her husband."

"Mrs. Adams's husband?"

"No, sir. This lady's husband. Her and him are staying at Miz Adams's."

"Are you sure, boy?"

"Yes, sir. I run errands for Miz Adams sometimes. She pays me three pennies each time I do something for her. This evening she had me go to the phar . . . phram . . . to the drug store. She wanted some sort of perscription picked up. So I did that. She had me take it upstairs to the room on the right hand side in back. A man came to the door there, then he got the lady for me to give the perscription bottle to. The lady was the one that Jimmy Doyle showed me a picture of just now. It was her, sir. I'm sure of it."

"You say she was with a man? Do you know who he is? What did he look like?"

"I never seen him before neither. He's, oh, not so tall. Doesn't look like much to me. He's kinda pale. Small. Rat-faced. And there was something wrong with his hair. Not from lice like mine was. His hair was kind of . . ."

"It was ragged and in patches, thick one place and not so thick in another?" Longarm suggested.

"Yes, sir, that's it exactly."

"Shit!"

"Oh. You already know who he is. Does that mean I won't be getting the reward money, sir?"

"If it was the girl I'm looking for that you saw, son, you'll sure get that reward. You have my word on it." Longarm turned to Harmon and said, "Tom, do me a favor, please, an' keep an eye on things here. We don't know for sure if this young man has the right girl in mind so sort out the reports for me while I'm over at this Mrs. Adams's house. Would you do that for me?"

"It will be a pleasure."

Longarm turned back to the boy. "Take me to the Adams place, son. Let's go see if you've found the right girl."

Chapter 32

If one of Jason's town constables was nearby Longarm could have been arrested as a Peeping Tom. He and the boy, whose name was Abraham, likely named for the former president, crouched behind a screen of junipers planted close around the two-story Adams house.

The place was every bit as large as the banker's fine home but was not nearly so elegant and certainly was not maintained to that high standard. Mrs. Adams's boarding house was seedy, the shingles cracked and curling and the whitewash that had once made it handsome was now pretty well washed away by the rains and the winds of passing seasons.

Longarm and Abe lurked beneath one of the windows on the side where there was no porch and they could kneel down close enough to hear the goings-on indoors. Longarm had chosen the open window of a room that was not lighted. If there was anything he did not need at the moment it was a neighbor or passerby spotting him in the glow of a lamp and sounding an alarm.

He considered himself lucky that Mrs. Adams did not have dogs. But then most boarding houses, certainly most of them that welcomed transients, avoided keeping dogs. The pets were too much trouble because of the day and night movement of strangers.

"Did you say the lady was sick?" Longarm whispered to the boy.

"She looked okay to me but maybe she was. I dunno."

"What was the prescription for, Abe? Do you remember?"

The kid shook his head. "I was just told to get her perscription. I dunno what was in it."

"And you took it to her when?"

Abe shrugged. "A couple hours ago. Maybe more. The drug store was still open but I think Mr. Carmody was about to close. Anyway, it's been a while. I just now was showed that picture of the lady and Jimmy told me where to find you."

"You did right, son," Longarm whispered.

He heard the creak of a spring then a pause and the slam of a screened door at the back of the house. Longarm motioned for Abe to stay where he was under the window while Longarm crawled quickly to the corner and peered into the backyard.

He got there in time to see Glenda Palmer open the door of the privy and let herself in.

Be damned, Longarm thought. The kid was right.

It was indeed Glenda.

And perhaps the most interesting thing about seeing her was what he was *not* seeing along with her.

Glenda was alone. No one was guarding her. She was not in irons or trussed up and being hidden away somewhere. She was free as a nightbird and could walk around to the street and right straight back to the Belton house.

If she damn well wanted to.

Obviously this girl had no intention of escaping. Seeing her here like this was proof enough of that.

Glenda was fully cooperating with her kidnappers.

Longarm pulled back from the corner of the house and lowered himself onto the chill, leaf-littered ground, positioning himself so he could continue to watch the outhouse without any likelihood of being spotted while he lay there.

Whatever Glenda was doing in there she was taking her time about it. That gave Longarm time to think.

Seeing Glenda's cooperation made a considerable change in things.

Obviously now the entire household here had to be considered as suspects in the kidnapping.

Obviously, too, Glenda's loyalties were subject to examination.

This phony kidnapping was an attempt to undermine her father's efforts in the United States Congress. She was trying to scuttle her own pa's entire political career with this trick.

Longarm considered the possibilities, then shook his head. The good thing was that once he got Glenda back to her mother it would be up to the politicians in Washington to worry about the details. And up to her father to straighten out his wayward daughter.

First, though, he had to get her back.

After what seemed a long time Glenda emerged from the privy. She returned to the porch and he could hear the trickle of water being poured into a tin basin, then some muted splashing while she washed her hands. Moments after that he again heard the creak and slam of the screen door.

Grimacing, Longarm came to his knees and then into a

crouch. He crept back along the side of the house to where Abe knelt. Whispering into the boy's ear he said, "I got another errand for you, son. I want you t' go find Constable Gilmore. You know him, don't you?"

"Yes, sir."

"Good. Go find Jason and tell him I need for him and all the policemen he can find to join me here. Tell him why. Can you do that, please?"

"Yes, sir, I can do that."

"Good." Longarm smiled. "You've already earned the reward. Find Jason for me and I'll pay you three cents for the errand, too."

Abe giggled and then slipped away, almost instantly blending into the shadows so that Longarm could no longer see him, not even knowing he was there.

The boy really should have been born an Indian, Longarm thought.

Longarm sat down and leaned against a foundation pier under the side of the house. All he could do now was wait for Jason and his coppers to show up, because he did not only want to recover Glenda, Longarm wanted to round up the rest of this gang, too, damn them.

Chapter 33

"Jason, if you don't mind . . . an' it's your department t' assign . . . but if you don't mind I'd sure appreciate you takin' the back door personally. We got . . . what? Five people here this morning not counting me and you? Fine. We'll need one on each side. Say you and one other guy busts open the back door an' leave one man to guard it. I'll keep one with me t' guard the front.

"I don't want one single swingin' dick to get away. Nor nary a fish factory neither."

"Excuse me," a very young Cheyenne policeman piped up. "What was that about fish?"

"I meant female, son."

The young fellow's expression showed that he clearly did not understand.

"Woman. Cunt. Pussy." Longarm sighed. "D'you mean you never sniff your damn finger after you had it up inside some girl's pussy? Smells like three-day-old fish, don't it? Well, that's what I was meaning. Don't let nobody, man nor woman, get outta this house without bein' taken into custody till we get the girl back an' sort this thing out."

The officer blushed a dark, mottled purple.

Longarm shook his head. They were getting younger every year it seemed like. "How's that sound to you, Jason?"

Gilmore nodded and began pointing at each man. "This side, please. That side for you, Jim. You and you come around back with me. You stay at the door to block it while Andy and me goes inside to flush out whoever is in there."

"That leaves me on the front door?" the young one said.

"That's right. I'm counting on you. Nobody goes out except we find every last soul inside there an' walk 'em all over to the jail to have a nice long chat about who they are an' what they know."

"I think we're ready," Jason said. "What is the signal to break in?"

"Me and the lad here will holler our fool heads off. When you hear that, come in snorting."

"Fine. Give us four minutes."

By way of an answer Longarm pulled his Ingersoll out of his vest pocket and looked down at the time. "All right, boys. We're on the clock an' counting."

"What's your name, son?"

"Terence, sir."

"Terry for short?"

"Yes, sir."

"Ever shoot a man, Terry?"

"No, sir."

Good Lord, Longarm thought. Was the whole damn Cheyenne police force composed of inexperienced youngsters? It was beginning to seem like it. "With any kind o' luck you won't have to shoot nobody today either, Terry. All I need for you t' do is to stand at the doorway . . . beside it, mind you, t' make sure nobody inside can throw a shot

162

through the open door an' catch you with it . . . just stand there with that shotgun and make sure nobody comes out.

"If anybody does make a run past you though, you got to shoot them, Terry. Man or woman, that don't matter. Anybody refuses to stop at your command, you shoot."

Terry looked decidedly uneasy at the prospect.

"Even if it means shooting them in the back, Terry. D'you understand that?"

"Yes, sir."

He looked like he was about to puke.

"Can I ask you somethin', Terry?"

"Yes, sir."

"What is it that you normally do?"

"On the force, you mean?"

Longarm nodded.

"I, uh, I handle the paperwork for the city jail, sir. I keep track of release dates, log in visitors, issue purchase orders for prisoner meals. Things like that."

"But you're a badge-wearin', sworn-to-serve police officer, aren't you?"

Terry grinned. "I guess I am now, sir."

Longarm managed to avoid rolling his eyes but he did turn his head away and under his breath mutter, "God help us all."

He looked down at his Ingersoll and grunted. "Our four minutes is up, Terry. Them other boys should be in place now, so on the count o' three the both of us are gonna scream our fool heads off. I'll snatch the door open. If it's locked, I'll point an' you can put a blast from that shooter into the lock. Both barrels. Right"—he leaned forward and pointed—"right here. But only if I tell you to. Then stand back because I'll be going in fast. You got all that?"

"Yes, sir. On three."

"Good," Longarm said. "Ready now. One . . . two . . ."

Chapter 34

Longarm let out a bull roar as he yanked the door open and charged inside with his revolver leveled. He was half afraid the kid might yank off a round and put a charge of buck into his back by accident, but Terry held his fire.

There were two men in the parlor, idling over coffee and a newspaper. Both of them threw their hands high when Longarm burst in on them.

"Here, mister, we ain't armed; take it all," one of them immediately shouted, reaching for a wallet and tossing it onto a small table beside his chair.

"Federal officer! Freeze," Longarm ordered. "This ain't a robbery, it's a raid so keep your hands up and don't reach for no gun or you'll be dead men, both o' you."

One of the two turned deathly pale and passed out cold with fright. The other sat bolt upright, his newspaper forgotten and his hands held over his head.

"Where's the girl?" Longarm demanded.

"We don't . . . uh . . . uh . . ." The fellow inclined his head toward the back of the house.

Longarm could hear more shouting back there and the

clatter of something falling. The would be Jason and his partner.

Keeping an eye on the two in the parlor, Longarm edged toward the kitchen. He met Jason in the hallway coming toward the front of the house. "Is everything under control? D'you have the girl?"

"I thought you would have her," Constable Gilmore said. "All we found back there was Mrs. Adams and the girl who helps her."

"Are you sure of the girl? Could it be Glenda Palmer that you have there?"

"No, I've known this girl since I was in short pants. She's local."

"What about . . ."

"Upstairs," Jason said.

"The delivery boy said her room is in the back of the house on the right."

Jason nodded.

"Let's go then. But watch yourself. We've already announced ourselves down here. Whoever is up there will be ready for us."

Longarm took the stairs two at a time, Jason Gilmore close behind with a shotgun in his hands.

The door Longarm wanted was closed. This time he did not bother trying the knob. He raised a boot and kicked the door hard beside the latch. The flimsy lock gave way and the door crashed open.

"Nobody move!" Longarm roared.

"Deputy Long. What *are* you doing here?"

Glenda Palmer stood beside a rumpled, unmade bed. The pretty girl appeared to be naked beneath the scant covering of a sheet that she snatched off the bed.

Damn fine legs, Longarm noticed. And other parts, too.

The room was empty except for . . . or was it. He held still and motioned for Jason to do the same. Something was not right here. He could hear . . . he could hear breathing, that's what. Very rapid. Panting almost. Frightened.

Longarm motioned the girl aside, then pointed first to Jason and next to Glenda Palmer, indicating Jason should watch her.

Longarm stepped into the room and, Colt at the ready, moved sideways around the perimeter keeping as far away from the bed as he could. When he reached the other side he could see the sole, the rather dirty sole, of a man's foot visible underneath the bed.

"You. Under the bed. D'you got a gun under there with you?"

There was no answer.

"You don't have t' say anything," Longarm said in a clear, firm voice, "but if you don't show yourself by the time I count to three I'm gonna start shooting t' blast you out from under there."

"Don't shoot! Please don't shoot."

"Come out then. Slow. Hands first an' those hands better be empty 'cause if I see a gun you're a dead man."

"I don't have a gun. Don't shoot."

"Nice an' slow, I said, an' your hands empty."

Despite the caution about coming out hands first, the first good look Longarm had was of a naked and rather hairy backside as the fellow slid facedown out from under the bed.

When he was out onto the floor he rolled over and, visibly trembling, sat up.

"Well, shit!" Longarm grumbled aloud. "What the hell are you doin' there?"

"I am . . . never mind what I am doing here."

"Who is he, Longarm?" Jason asked.

"You can put your gun away. This miserable little weasel is a reporter of some sort though God knows who'd be dumb enough t' hire somebody like him."

"You know him then?"

"He's been dogging the Palmers since Denver that I know of. I wouldn't know about before they got there." Longarm shoved his Colt back into the leather and thought about kicking Sebastian Brewer in the nuts just to get his attention. The little sonuvabitch was lucky Longarm was a representative of the Untied States government or he would have gotten that kick. And maybe worse.

Something of that desire must have showed in Longarm's eyes because Brewer hunched over, his hands moving to cover himself, and he backed away from Longarm as far as he could go, ending up pressed against a tall chest that stood against the wall. "Don't touch me," he said, "or I'll sue."

"I'm damn sure gonna touch you when I snap the handcuffs on you. Now put your clothes on."

"You can't make me . . ."

"No, but I can cuff you and drag your sorry ass over to the jail dressed just the way you are right now."

"You can't arrest me."

"The hell I can't. The charge is kidnapping. You aren't gonna walk free for twenty, twenty-five years. By the time you get out of prison, Brewer, a little piece o' shit like you, you're gonna walk bowlegged an' dribble brown everywhere you go from all the dicks you will have had shoved up your ass for all them years."

"I haven't . . ."

"Oh, no!" Glenda yelped. "Sabby didn't kidnap me,

168

Marshal. We love each other. We're going to be married. Didn't Mama show you the note I sent to her?"

"The only note she got, girl, was a kidnap note saying your pa should forget about his Indian land reforms or you'd wind up dead."

"No, that can't be right. I wrote the note out in my own hand, five pages of it, telling Mama not to worry, that I was to marry the man of my dreams."

"If you did, girl, then somebody got rid o' your note an' substituted one o' their own. Looks like Sebastian here kidnapped you without you even knowin' it."

"No, I . . . I never," Brewer declared. "I'm innocent. I love her."

"Feel free t' tell that to the jury when you go on trial for kidnapping," Longarm told him. "Now get dressed."

"You can't arrest him, Marshal. Really."

"Glenda, I can arrest you right along with him if I think you been an accomplice in a crime. Now I'd suggest you best get dressed, too. We'll have somebody take you back t' your mother while me and Sebastian here go get him a nice, comfortable start on viewing the world from inside jail cell bars. Jason, you take the girl, will you, please? An' it will be my pleasure t' lock Mr. Brewer away."

Chapter 35

Longarm sat with his boots propped on the edge of the police chief's polished walnut desk, trimming his fingernails
with a pocket knife, smoke curling past his eyes from a
tasty cheroot. For the past twenty minutes or so he had
been listening to Sebastian Brewer weep and wail and
gnash his teeth from the inside of a jail cell.

Brewer loudly and constantly protested his innocence.
Longarm quietly and persistently ignored him.

The front door opened and Jason Gilmore came in.

"How'd it go at the house?" Longarm asked.

Jason shrugged. "The mother is falling all over herself
with joy to have her baby back. The object of all this concern is pissed off because she got dragged away from her
one true love and hauled back to her mama."

In the cell Brewer shut up and listened to what the lawmen were saying.

"How'd a nasty little turd like that get her drawer down
anyway?" Longarm asked.

"It seems our boy Sebastian is literary minded. He
talked with her about French literature and some SOB
named B.O. Wolf."

"That is Beowulf, you clod," Brewer shouted.

"See what I mean," Jason said. He glanced back toward Brewer and spat. "Asshole." The prisoner shut up and sat down.

"I been thinking," Longarm said. "I want you to handle the charges against this boy."

"Fine. I won't mind getting some credit, but why should I do the filing instead of you?"

"If I charge him a good lawyer might get the kidnapping prosecuted under federal statutes. If I remember rightly the most he could draw for kidnap would be twenty years. With time off for good behavior he could make it out of the pen in fifteen, sixteen years or thereabouts. If his asshole holds out an' some jealous he-bitch don't murder him first." Longarm took a slow drag on his cheroot and dropped his boots to the floor.

He said, "If you charge him, Jason, it'll be under local law, and in Wyoming Territory kidnapping is a hanging offense. The way I see it, we'd kinda be doing the little piece o' shit a favor by getting him hanged. It'd save him years of spreading his ass cheeks or sucking cocks while he's in prison."

"The girl swears she wasn't kidnapped," Jason put in. "She told her mama that when I took her back."

"I still have that note in my pocket," Longarm said. "Just because the girl didn't *know* she was bein' kidnapped don't mean that she *wasn't* kidnapped. A jury won't have no trouble seein' that an' sending our boy Sebastian to the gallows."

"Oh, God!" Brewer wailed. "But I didn't . . . didn't mean for this to go so far."

"Didn't intend t' hang?" Longarm shot back, sarcasm thick in his voice. "That's the first true thing I've heard

172

come outta your mouth. Tell me somethin', boy. You like the taste o' cum, do you? You'd better 'cause you are gonna drink a lot of it before you hang."

"Oh, Jesus!"

Gilmore gave the prisoner a withering look. "He may well save your soul, mister, but your ass is going to hang. Now shut up or we will buck and gag you to keep you quiet."

Sebastian Brewer began to cry. Literally. Tears rolled down his cheeks leaving wet, glistening tracks behind.

"Brave bastard, ain't he?" Longarm observed dispassionately.

"I . . . I . . . I can help you," Brewer wailed.

"You can help us stretch a rope, that's what you can help us with," Longarm told him.

Jason helped himself to some coffee from the pot on the stove and sat across the desk from Longarm. "Did you know there are people back East who will pay a small fortune for a hangman's noose that has been used. They pay even more if you include a photograph of the hanged man and what you call a Certificate of Authenticity. I'm thinking to have me some pictures taken when they hang *asshole* there." He hooked a thumb toward Brewer and took a sip of the steaming hot coffee. "You want some of this?" he offered.

"No thanks," Longarm said, reaching forward to stub his cigar butt out in the police chief's ashtray.

"Please," Brewer howled. "I can help you. Really."

"You got nothing to say that we want t' hear," Longarm said dismissively.

"I can tell you who paid me to kidnap the girl."

Longarm looked at Jason Gilmore, then at Sebastian Brewer. "I thought you didn't kidnap her."

"I did. I admit it. I can tell you all about it. But first you have to promise to let me go."

Longarm turned away again and said to Jason, "Some guys just got no grasp of reality, you know that?"

"Wait," Brewer begged. "I can . . . just promise I won't hang. You'll talk to the judge. Maybe get me a reduced sentence. How about that?"

Longarm pursed his lips and pondered the request for a moment, then he nodded. "We might do that. No death sentence and a recommendation to whatever judge you draw. No promises, mind. That ain't our place to give. But we could put in a recommendation for some sort o' leniency."

"And I wouldn't hang?"

"Yeah, I think we can safely promise that much," Longarm said.

Jason nodded. "If we file charges against you in federal court we could guarantee it," he said.

"You would do that? You swear it?"

"Yeah. Maybe. If you have something worthwhile t' tell us."

"I . . . oh, Jesus."

Longarm looked away. "Talk. Hang. Your choice." He winked at Jason Gilmore and waited for Sebastian Brewer to open up.

Did they really hang kidnappers in Wyoming Territory? he wondered. The truth was that he had no idea whether they did or not.

"Let me tell you how it was," Brewer babbled. "I can tell you everything."

Chapter 36

Jason Gilmore shook his head. "You didn't see her with her mother this evening, Longarm. I tell you, that girl is not going to believe us when we tell her how this scum took advantage and mistreated her."

"Mistreated hell," Brewer complained. "She was no virgin when I got to her. And for that matter, she's pretty but she's a lousy lay. She doesn't move her hips much and she won't take it in her mouth."

"Shut up, shithead," Longarm advised, "or I'll belt you one in *your* mouth."

"She will believe," Jason said, "if she hears it from his mouth."

Longarm shrugged. "We're going over there anyway. I suppose we could drag him along and let him offer his apologies an' explanations to the girl an' to her mama."

"I'll do that, Marshal. I can convince her. But I won't . . . you know . . . I won't embarrass her in front of her mother by saying anything about her not being a virgin or about her being such a piss-poor piece of ass."

"Damned generous of you, Brewer. All right. Turn around so's we can put the cuffs on you."

"Can't you put them on with my hands in front? It hurts when you pull my arms back and cuff me behind my back."

"Turn around, asshole. If it hurts that's your problem."

"Yes, sir."

Two minutes later they were out the door and on their way to the Belton house.

Despite the late hour the place was lighted as bright as a Fourth of July carnival. It was obvious that the entire household was awake and active now that Glenda had been safely returned. Well, more or less safely. It was common knowledge by now that she had been found naked and in bed with an equally naked man. That information would not do her reputation much good.

Longarm led their little procession with a shotgun-wielding Jason Gilmore at the tail end and Sebastian Brewer in the middle. As they reached the house and let themselves in through the gate Longarm could hear a woman's voice inside announcing their approach to whoever was inside.

"Now mind your manners, asshole," Longarm snarled as they mounted the steps to the porch.

The maidservant Maria met them at the door and motioned for them to come in. Longarm removed his hat and stepped inside, the others following.

The four of them, Maria leading, went into the parlor where they found Elspeth Palmer and Glenda along with Idamae Belton and several other hatchet-faced middle-aged women—suffragettes who were sympathetic to the cause, he guessed—and even the cook Martha. All of them, Longarm suspected, would be hoping for juicy gossip that they could embellish and pass along in the days and weeks to come.

"Why did you bring that . . . that *creature* here?" Elspeth demanded.

176

"This creature wants t' save his neck by confessing to what he done, an' it's likely that Glenda there will understand an' believe when she hears it all from his own mouth."

"I love him!" Glenda wailed. "I wanted to run away with him."

"Yeah, honey, but ol' Sebastian here loves money more'n he loves you. He was paid to kidnap you. Wasn't you, asshole?" Longarm nudged Brewer in the back, then crossed the room to stand beside Glenda. "This wasn't your fault, girl. But you was kidnapped for sure an' we got the note to prove it. A note that was inside an envelope that you addressed with your own hand."

"I will listen, but I know that he loves me just as I love him."

"You can't believe that," Elspeth snapped.

"I do, Mother."

"It's true," Brewer put in. "I do love her. Truly I do, Glen. You have to believe that."

"Oh, I do, darling, I do." She started to rise from her chair, heading toward Brewer. "I do love you." Longarm put his hand on her shoulder to hold her away from the prisoner.

"But I have to tell you the truth, dear," Brewer said. "I want to make a clean breast of it and I want you to understand. Marshal Long told it straight. I was paid to take you. It was only after I met you that I fell in love with you. I never meant to hurt you."

Again Glenda started forward but this time she was stopped by a thunderclap noise, a gout of flame, shattered glass and billowing curtains as someone just outside fired a shotgun through a side window.

Women screamed. Both Brewer and Jason Gilmore were knocked off their feet.

Longarm did not take time to examine their wounds although a quickly spreading red stain proved that at least one of them was injured.

He ducked and again the shotgun outside that window bellowed, sending a pattern of shots rattling against the handsome flocked wallpaper that decorated the Belton parlor.

The second shot shattered a lamp on an end table, spraying flaming oil over the table and felling a rocking chair beside it.

Longarm hit the floor, rolled and came up with Jason's double-barrel L.C. Smith in his hands. He thumbed back the hammer and sent the first charge of buckshot blindly through the window to discourage whoever was out there.

It would have been suicidal to gallop through that window himself when he knew there was an assassin just outside. Instead he crossed the room in long, swift strides and threw open the sash of the front window.

He stepped out onto the porch, shotgun still in his hands, and crept as silently as he could to the side where the shots were fired from.

Whoever was there had enough time to reload by now and a load of buck in the face can fuck up a man's whole day. Instead of sticking his head around the corner of the house Longarm dropped to his belly, took his hat off and risked a quick look.

He could see a man's shape, very dim in the little bit of flickering light that escaped through the broken window.

The man raised the shotgun again. He was on tiptoes, standing atop a crate or box of some sort to put him high enough to see inside the house. He seemed to be taking aim at someone inside.

That was more than enough for Longarm.

He shoved Jason's shotgun around the corner of the building, cocked the other barrel and found the back trigger.

The Smith bucked hard against his shoulder and smacked his cheek hard enough to likely give him a shiner.

A dozen feet away he could hear the dull thump of a body striking the earth.

Longarm came to his feet. He had no more shells for the scattergun so he dropped it, clattering loudly on the porch floorboards, and drew his Colt.

If the assassin was still alive. . . .

Stealth was damn sure out of the question now. Longarm took a deep breath, steeled his nerve and with as loud an unnerving roar as he could manage leaped off the porch with his revolver poised.

He did not need to shoot again. The charge of buckshot had done its work almighty well. The assassin was himself assassinated. So to speak.

He was damn sure dead, his belly torn open and chest shattered.

None of the lead pellets had struck his face however and he was still a handsome, even a dignified-looking corpse.

"Well I'll be a sonuvabitch," Longarm mumbled.

Then, remembering, he dashed back inside to help extinguish the fire that had been started in the parlor.

Chapter 37

"You shouldn't feel bad. It ain't your fault. None of it," Longarm murmured into the soft flesh of a pink-tipped tit.

"It is my fault," she protested.

"No it ain't," he insisted. "You couldn't of known."

"But why . . . ?"

"Money," Longarm told her. "The stockholders are having an audit done but I can already tell you that Banker Belton was invested too heavy in livestock loans to cowmen and sheepherders. If the Indian land use regulations get changed an' they hafta pay market rates for their grazing rights, most of them are likely to default on their loans. Belton was worried the bank could be foreclosed an' sold out from under him. The son of a bitch was moving money back an' forth fast as a juggler in a traveling wagon show. If anybody defaulted he'd be in deep shit his own self. He couldn't afford t' have those land rights laws changed. Not that they likely will be no matter how much yelping and groaning they do back in Washington. The cowmen got themselves a lot o' power back there. They won't let none of it happen. There wasn't need for him t' get so scared as to try an' force things with his stupid kidnapping plan."

"Were any others in on it?" She began nibbling the tip of his cock and tickling the sensitive patch between the base of his balls and his asshole. After a moment she moved around and began licking him there.

"Prob'ly," Longarm said.

She lifted her head. "What? I couldn't hear you with your legs clamped around my ears like that."

Longarm grinned and used two fingers to lift her hair and push it over onto the other side of her head so he could get a better look at her. "I said we'll never know if there was others involved or if Belton done it all on his own."

"Does that matter?"

"Not t' me. Does it to you?"

She shook her head.

"An' if it matters to your daddy it's up to him t' work it out. I done what I was supposed t' do."

Glenda smiled. "You may have done what Daddy wanted of you but I am not through with you, mister. Not by a long shot. Now if you wouldn't mind, I could enjoy a little of that sixty-nine thing you taught me before you put this pole where it belongs."

"Glad to oblige, miss, always glad to oblige a lady." He waited until she had his cock sunk wetly inside her mouth, then pulled the girl's body to him.

He smiled as he thought about how much longer this suffragette speaking tour still had to run. And it was Custis Long's sworn duty to accompany the two Palmer women every minute of it.

Glenda toyed lightly with his balls while she sucked him deep inside her pretty mouth. Uh huh! Not bad duty at all.

Watch for

**LONGARM AND THE
PANTHER MOUNTAIN SHOOT-OUT**

the 337th novel in the exciting LONGARM
series from Jove

Coming in December!

Explore the exciting Old West with one of the men who made it wild!

GIANT-SIZED ADVENTURE FROM AVENGING ANGEL LONGARM.

Longarm and the Outlaw Empress

0-515-14235-2

When Deputy U.S. Marshal Custis Long stops a stagecoach robbery, he tracks the bandits to a town called Zamora. A haven for the lawless, it's ruled by one of the most powerful, brilliant, and beautiful women in the West...a woman whom Longarm will have to face, up close and personal.

**GIANT-SIZED ADVENTURE FROM
AVENGING ANGEL LONGARM.**

Longarm and the
Undercover Mountie
0-515-14017-1

This all-new, giant-sized adventure in the popular all-action
series puts the "wild" back in the Wild West.

U.S. Marshal Custis Long and Royal Canadian Mountie
Sergeant Foster have an evil town to clean up—where
outlaws indulge their wicked ways. But first, they'll have to
stay ahead of the meanest vigilante committee anybody
ever ran from.

9